I SPY WITH MY PSYCHIC EYE SOMEONE DEAD

PIPER ASHWELL PSYCHIC P.I., BOOK 8

KELLY HASHWAY

To Ayla with love

CHAPTER ONE

It's Friday night, which means I should be home, sitting on my couch with my adorable golden retriever, Jezebel, and reading a good book. But somehow, I'm in a fancy restaurant with my partner, Detective Mitchell Brennan. I'm still not sure how I went from hating the man my father forced me to work with to calling him my boyfriend.

"You're doing it again, aren't you?" Mitchell asks me.

"Doing what?"

"Wondering how you got so lucky." He smirks.

I roll my eyes. "It's like you're the psychic one, not me." I make sure to lace my words with as much sarcasm as is humanly possible. If only I'd seen this coming. I'm not a gifted clairvoyant, though. Sure, I've had a few premonitions, but my talents lay in psychometry, reading the energy off objects. It's how I pay my bills as a psychic P.I. It's also why I try to avoid physical contact with other people. Sometimes it's harder for me not to read someone or something than it is *to* read them. That's another reason why I tried to avoid getting into a relationship with Mitchell, who used to date more women in a single week than books I can read in a month, and given my lack of social life, that's saying a lot. He's changed, though.

Out of the corner of my eye, a motion draws my attention. Our waiter, a guy named Austin, according to his name tag, is wiping up some wine he spilled two tables over and apologizing profusely to the man he nearly covered with Merlot.

Mitchell leans forward on the table, and his gaze flits in the waiter's direction. "Why do you seem more interested in our waiter than in me?"

"Don't you think he seems jumpy?" I ask, noticing the way the waiter keeps looking around the dining room.

"Are your senses picking up on something?" All hint of jealousy is gone from his tone. He's in full-on detective mode now.

"I don't know." Maybe I'm just not handling this dating thing. It took me a long time to admit my feelings for Mitchell and even longer to get used to the idea that he's my boyfriend. It's possible being in a fancy restaurant, which is not my scene at all, is too much for me and my mind is creating a distraction to put me at ease. It says a lot that a possible person in trouble is more normal and comforting to me than being on a date with a man I actually care about.

"Piper Rose Ashwell," Mitchell says, "are you trying to find a way to end our date early?"

I meet his gaze. "FYI, the three-name call is reserved for my parents. Using it will not only end this date early but will ensure there won't be any future dates as well."

Mitchell bobs his head. "Duly noted. Now, tell me what's really bothering you. Is it all the people?"

Mitchell purposely reserved this table in the back corner so I wouldn't be surrounded by people while I eat. He tries to accommodate all my shortcomings and quirks, but I'm still way out of my comfort zone.

When I don't respond, he flags down the waiter.

"Yes, sir?" Austin asks, ringing his hands in front of him. What is he so anxious about? I could easily find out by "accidentally" touching his hand and sparking a vision, but I don't think reading the waiter is proper date behavior.

"Could we get our food to go, please?" Mitchell removes his wallet from his pocket and pulls out his credit card.

"Certainly, sir. No problem." The waiter takes the card, looks around the dining room for the hundredth time, and then hurries to the kitchen.

I lean toward Mitchell and whisper, "You saw that, right?"

"Yeah, I saw it." Mitchell scans the dining room. "Do you think he's afraid of being fired? Maybe his boss is keeping an eye on him. He did just spill wine at that table over there. It's possible he's been screwing up a lot lately, and he's fearful of losing his job."

It's possible, but I can't help feeling there's more to it.

Mitchell reaches across the table and places his hand on top of my left hand. He's always careful not to touch my right hand so I don't accidentally read him. I've never known why I can only read people and objects with my right hand, but that's the way it's been since I discovered my psychic abilities at the age of twelve. "Maybe I'm pushing for too much too soon. Fancy dinners aren't your thing. I'm totally fine with eating takeout on your couch with Jezebel."

I smirk. "I notice you didn't mention me in that equation."

He bobs one shoulder. "Eventually, you were going to figure out I'm only dating you for your dog. It might as well come out now."

"Oh, I've known from day one your interest in me is solely to get to Jezebel. I can't blame you either."

He squeezes my hand but quickly lets go when Austin returns with our food, which he's bagged for us. He hands Mitchell the check to sign.

I take the time to study Austin. The guy is more than a little jumpy, and it's not in an "I don't want to lose my job" kind of way. He's scared of something. No. He's scared of someone. I look around the dining room and open up my senses at the same time, hoping to get a feel of anyone who might wish ill upon the waiter.

The only one who seems upset with him is the man whose wine Austin spilled. The guy's emotions are radiating a sense of disgust at the waiter's incompetence, though. Nothing more.

"Piper?" Mitchell says, and I realize we're alone at the table and Mitchell is already on his feet with the food in hand. "Did I miss a vision?"

"No. Nothing like that." I stand up, placing the napkin from my lap on the table next to my untouched water glass. "I'm all set."

Mitchell walks around the table and places his hand on the small of my back to escort me out of the restaurant. As we pass the kitchen, my senses zero in on Austin, who is whispering into his cell phone.

"Just a few more days, please. That's all I'm asking for." He runs a hand through his dark hair, which is tousled as if he's already performed this action several times in the last few minutes.

"Think he's begging for his job?" Mitchell whispers to me as we head for the exit.

No. That call has nothing to do with his job. That much I'm certain of. But seeing as I've already derailed our date, I keep my opinions to myself and just shrug.

Jezebel is excited to see us back so soon from dinner. Thankfully, she puts a big smile on Mitchell's face since I officially ruined our first fancy dinner out. I really am not cut out for dating. I go to the kitchen and brew some toasted almond coffee for after we eat our meals. Mitchell gets utensils, napkins, and drinks and sets it all up on the coffee table. I'm surprised when he doesn't turn on the television, which only ever gets put on when he's here. I much prefer to read, but Mitchell's pointed out that it's rude to read when someone is trying to talk to you. I admit to having a book on the side table for when he excuses himself to the bathroom. I'm a work in progress.

"How's your mushroom ravioli?" Mitchell asks.

To be honest, I'm not sure I'm even tasting my food right now. My mind is focused on that waiter and what I was feeling at the restaurant. I don't want to tell Mitchell that, though, after I already ruined our date, so instead I say, "Would you like some?"

He leans away from me. "Did Piper Ashwell just offer to share her food?"

"Is that weird?" I ask, wondering if I just committed some new relationship blunder I'm not aware of.

"For you, yes. You usually fight me for food."

I force a laugh because that's totally true. We fight over the pastries from Marcia's Nook on a daily basis. "I'm not all that hungry, and there's plenty here. Help yourself." I push my plate closer to his.

He eyes me suspiciously. "I'm not sure if this is a test or not."

"Stop reading into things so much. If you want to try some, go ahead. It's as simple as that." When he still doesn't react, I fork a ravioli from my plate and put it on his. "There. Problem solved."

Mitchell takes a bit of the ravioli, and his face scrunches up. "Piper, that's not mushroom ravioli. That's lobster ravioli. The waiter gave you the wrong order."

"He did?" I cut off a piece of the ravioli and pop it into my mouth. Sure enough, now that I'm actually paying attention to what I'm eating, I taste the lobster. "Weird."

"What's weird is how you ate several raviolis and had no clue it was the wrong order." He puts his fork down and shifts on the couch so he's facing me. "What's really going on? Is all of this too much for you? Is that the problem?"

Instead of facing him and having an adult conversation, I clutch my fork like it's a lifeline and stare at my plate of food. "I don't know what it was, but I couldn't help sensing something was very off about our waiter. My mind is still focused on him."

"He's a terrible waiter. That much is clear after he spilled wine and screwed up your order. Why do you think it's something more? Did you have a vision?"

"No. I don't know what it is. I just..." I can't explain it.

Mitchell reaches for the fork in my hand, removing it from my clenched fingers and placing it on my plate. "Piper, look at me."

I raise my eyes to meet his gaze.

"Is it possible tonight took you too far out of your comfort zone and you tried to console yourself by creating a problem with the waiter so you had something else to focus on?"

Great, Mitchell thinks he's my therapist now. I let out a deep breath.

He holds up a hand. "I'm not trying to psychoanalyze you. I just want you to be okay with us, so if you're not, you need to tell me. You haven't had any premonitions about things ending badly for us, have you?"

I can't blame him for asking since it's possible I lied and told him exactly that to avoid dating him in the first place, but I also thought I'd accepted the fact that I have feelings for him despite my best efforts not to.

I can't come up with anything to say that won't make him upset, so I settle for, "I think maybe I'm just tired."

He frowns, making it clear he doesn't buy that excuse for a second, but he gets up and goes to the kitchen, where he pours the coffee I brewed. But he doesn't pour two cups.

"Where's yours?" I ask when he returns with my mug.

He sighs and stares down at me, not retaking his seat. "I'm going home."

"Mitchell, you don't have to leave." Even before we started dating, he'd stay at my place until I went to bed.

"I think it's best if I do. Drink your coffee and call it an early night. Hopefully, you'll feel better in the morning."

He's letting me off the hook, and I'm not sure I like it. "You're upset with me, aren't you?" I ask.

He shakes his head. "I'm really not. We both knew this would take some getting used to."

Then why is he handling it so much better than I am?

"Do you have plans tomorrow?" I ask.

He grabs his plate and brings it to the kitchen. "Actually, I do. I'm helping Wallace with a case."

"Oh. Okay." I don't call him out on the fact that my senses are tingling, screaming that he's lying to me. I know what he's doing. He's giving me space because he thinks that's what I want. "Maybe you can stop by when you're finished. I was planning to order a calzone for dinner."

Jez barks at the mention of calzone, one of her favorite meals. I swear she understands everything I say.

Mitchell smiles at her as he brings his to-go container to the door. "I'll call you if it's not too late."

I nod. Jezebel rushes over to Mitchell, who bends down to kiss her head. She reciprocates by licking his chin.

"Take good care of your mommy, Jez," he tells her. He stands up. "Sweet dreams, Piper."

"Thanks for dinner," I say because I don't know how to apologize for my behavior this evening. I've never sent him running like this before.

He gives a small nod before leaving.

Jez comes over and jumps up on the couch next to me. "I guess it's just us girls tonight." She puts her head in my lap and stares up at me with her big brown eyes. "I'm sorry I chased him away on you. Maybe one day Mommy will figure out how to act like a normal human being."

Jez sits up and licks my cheek.

"Thanks, sweet girl. I know you love me just the way I am."

I pack up the rest of my food, convinced Mitchell is right and I was trying to read more into the waiter's behavior than was actually there because I was uncomfortable being on a real date. "Let's go to bed and try to forget this night happened," I tell Jez.

Hopefully, Mitchell will be willing to put it behind us, too.

CHAPTER TWO

Monday morning I'm fuming as I walk into my office. Mitchell blew me off for the entire weekend. I got one lame text each day about how he's busy working on a case with Officer Wallace. Dad took the day off since he and Mom went away for a long weekend to celebrate their anniversary. So, I'm sitting in my office, staring at the door, waiting to see if Mitchell will show his face or avoid me today as well.

I'm about to get up and go next door to Marcia's Nook for some coffee and to vent to Marcia about all of this when Mitchell waltzes in with a file in his hand. "You're not going to believe this," he says.

"Believe what?" I ask. "That my boyfriend lied to me about working a case all weekend because he doesn't want to admit he's upset with me?"

He stops in front of my desk and lets out a long breath. "I figured you'd sense I was lying."

"Yet you did it anyway. Why?"

He tosses the file folder onto my desk and rubs the back of his neck. "I don't know. I guess I thought I was doing us both a favor by making up an excuse to give you space."

"If I wanted space, I'd tell you. You should know that by now." I'm not exactly the type to hide my feelings. At least not well.

He stares down at me. "You really did sense something was off about the waiter. I know that now."

I cock my head at him. "What are you talking about?"

He dips his head in the direction of the file folder. "See for yourself."

I reach for the folder with my left hand and open it up. A crime scene photo is the first thing my eyes land on. It's the waiter from Friday night. He's seated in the driver's seat of a car, and there's a bullet hole in his forehead. I slam the file closed and push it away from me. "Damn it." I couldn't be angrier with myself. "I dismissed the feeling I got because I thought you were right. I thought I was freaking out about us and it was making my senses go crazy."

Mitchell finally sits down. "I'm sorry about that. It's my fault you didn't listen to your senses. I was sure I had pushed you too far. I should have believed you when you said something at the restaurant." He sits forward, resting his elbows on his thighs and hanging his head. "I'm an idiot."

"You are, but this one is on me. I know better than to dismiss a feeling. I should have dug deeper and tried to foresee this happening." I pull the folder back to me and scan the rest of the file. His name was Austin Hawkins. He was twenty-four years old. He'd been employed at that restaurant for six years, having worked there while going to college. "If I had even tried to read him, I would have known he wasn't a new employee who kept screwing up and was afraid of being fired. He was nervous because he knew someone was after him."

Mitchell raises his head. "Fact?"

I nod. Sometimes things just come to me, and without knowing why, I can be certain they're true. "We need to find out who did this and why," I say.

"There's a problem with that plan," he says.

"What? No leads?" That's typically when Mitchell brings a case to me, which is where my abilities come in.

"More like no case," he says. "It's been assigned to Officer Andrews. I'm not on it."

Officer Andrews is the one officer at the Weltunkin PD who not only doesn't believe in what I do but absolutely hates me. Granted, I did discover his affair when I read him against his will, and I might have also been the reason he was suspended from the police force. Of course, none of that would have happened if he treated me like a human being. "When did he get back from his suspension?"

"Today. Chief Johansen thought it would be best to give him a case to keep him busy and get him back on track."

And, thanks to my stellar good luck, it had to be *this* case. The case where I personally feel responsible for not helping the victim. "I have to work this. I owe it to Austin Hawkins after I did nothing to prevent this." I'm about to totally lose it, and Mitchell must sense it because he says, "That's why I took the case file. Austin's mother lives with him. If we can get her to hire your P.I. Agency, you can look into this case, and Andrews won't be able to stop you."

"What about you?" I ask, knowing there's no way Officer Andrews will allow Mitchell to work the case alongside him.

"I'll have to help you around any other cases I get in the meantime. It's not a perfect solution, but Chief Johansen knows how Andrews and I feel about each other. He's not going to allow us to team up on this one. It's too risky."

Because Chief Johansen knows it would only impede the investigation. "So, I'm on my own."

"Only for the morning. I'll catch up with you at lunchtime."

"You're leaving?" I stand up. All the emotions and

energy inside me are about to burst out, and I'm not sure in what form.

"I have to go to the station. But, Piper, I really am sorry about Friday night and this weekend. I should have listened to you, and I shouldn't have run off like that. I handled it really badly."

I shrug. "We both totally suck at relationships. In a way, I feel better that I'm not the only one acting like an idiot."

He laughs. "We do make quite the pair, don't we?"

"Jez missed you."

"Is she the only one who missed me?" He dips his head and gives me a small smile.

"Hmm." I squint up at the ceiling like I'm trying to recall if anyone else missed him. "My dad did ask about you once on Sunday, so it's possible he missed you a little bit."

Mitchell takes my hand and tugs me to him. "You missed me. I know you did because you love to argue with me."

"That I do."

"I've got to go. Call me and let me know where you'll be at lunchtime so I can meet up with you to work on the case."

"Will do." I use my phone to snap a picture of the case file before handing it back to Mitchell.

He gives my hand a quick squeeze before leaving.

Since it's not in my best interest to talk to a potential

client without being fully caffeinated, I walk the twenty-three steps to Marcia's Nook, my favorite bookstore that also happens to have an amazing café. Marcia looks up and smiles at me when the bell above the door chimes.

"Good morning, Piper," she says.

I look around at the empty café. "Where is everyone?"

"You just missed the morning crowd." She's already pouring my large toasted almond coffee.

"Happy to hear it," I say, scanning the bakery display.

"Are your dad and Mitchell joining you this morning?" she asks, capping my to-go cup.

"No. Dad and Mom are still away for their anniversary, and Mitchell is at the station."

"Does that mean you don't have a case to work on?"

"Not yet. I'm going to see about one after I leave here."

She gestures to the display case. "The cranberry-orange muffins are still hot if you're interested."

"Yes, please," I say, taking out my phone to pay.

She rings me up, but I can tell she has something on her mind. "Do you want to talk about what's bothering you?" she finally asks.

I take the pastry bag and coffee. I should have known she'd pick up on my sour mood. "I dismissed a feeling I had, and now someone is dead because of it."

She cocks her head at me. "I have a hard time believing you had a premonition of someone's death and didn't think anything of it."

"No, it's nothing like that. Mitchell and I were at

dinner Friday night, and I felt like something was wrong with our waiter. I didn't know what, and I didn't bother to look deeper into the feeling."

She leans on the counter. "So, nothing told you his life was in danger?"

"Well, no, but I knew something was wrong."

"Piper, there's a difference between thinking something might be wrong and thinking someone is going to die. Is it possible you're being too hard on yourself?"

I shake my head. "I let the awkwardness from being on a date where I was totally uncomfortable take away from my ability to see what I should have. The waiter was so jumpy. I should have tried to find out why."

"Are you saying anytime a complete stranger seems nervous it's your responsibility to find out why?" she asks. Even though she's only a few years older than I am, she has the ability to look at me like she's my mother. Only I'm much more amused by the look when Marcia gives it to me than when my actual mother does.

"I see your point, but the fact that my senses zeroed in on him should have told me to pay closer attention. Instead, I left the restaurant."

"Probably at Mitchell's suggestion because he thought you were uncomfortable in the public setting and would rather be at home."

She knows us both so well.

She stands up straight. "I've said it before, and I'll say it again. You expect too much from yourself sometimes."

"Excuse me?" a voice comes from behind me. "I have to get to work, and I'd really like to buy this book first."

I turn around to see a tall, muscular man holding a book. "I'm sorry. I didn't mean to hold you up." I step aside. "Thanks, Marcia."

"Anytime, Piper. Good luck with the case."

I smile before leaving. Once I'm in my Mazda, I pull up the address for Mrs. Hawkins from the photo I took of Austin's case file. I know the road she lives on, so I buckle up and head there, hoping against all odds that Officer Andrews won't be there when I arrive.

The house is an old Victorian on a road where most of the homes were built quite some time ago and in need of updating. I pull into the driveway, which is thankfully empty—meaning I don't have to worry about Officer Andrews being inside. Of course, he could show up before I leave, so I'm not in the clear just yet.

In front of the garage is a freestanding basketball hoop that seems very out of place with the rest of the house, which has a distinctly old feel to it. I get out of the car and walk up to the front door. I hate introducing myself as a psychic P.I., and until I get a read on Mrs. Hawkins, I plan to withhold the "psychic" part of my introduction. I ring the doorbell, and I'm a little surprised when the door swings open immediately.

"Can I help you?" asks a woman who appears to be in her early fifties with graying hair and glasses.

"Actually, I'm hoping to help you. I'm Piper Ashwell, a private investigator here in town."

"I didn't call a private investigator," she says.

"I know. I actually work closely with the Weltunkin PD." Okay, so I'm conveniently leaving off the part where I'm not exactly working with the police on her son's case. "I believe I can be of assistance in finding out what happened to your son." I try to keep my voice as sympathetic as possible. Dad's usually the one who's good with potential clients.

"Oh, well I talked to the police already."

"Yes, I'm aware," I lie. "But I was hoping I could speak with you as well. If you're not too busy," I add, knowing she won't want to say she's too busy to help find her son's killer.

"Please come in." She opens the door wider to allow me to enter.

Despite the home being large, it feels small since all the rooms are completely sectioned off from each other—another sign of the home's age. She directs me to the living room off to our right.

"Could I get you something to drink?" she asks.

"No, thank you. I'm fine. I'd rather get right to the investigation."

"Of course."

She sits down in a high-backed chair, and I take a seat on the floral print couch.

"When did you last see your son?" I ask.

"Sunday morning. Well, I guess it was actually afternoon. He had just woken up and was late to his poker game." She lowers her head and laces her hands in her lap. "He had somewhat of a gambling problem. I kept begging him not to throw his money away like that, but he's an adult. There really wasn't anything I could do to stop him."

I nod in understanding. "Does he play poker every Sunday afternoon?"

"Unfortunately. But it didn't end with poker. He bet on just about everything. Horseracing, football games, basketball games, you name it. He watched every sport under the sun. He even started betting on professional wrestling, and we all know those matches are rigged." She sighs, and then her disapproval is replaced with grief as sobs shake her upper body. "I'm sorry. I just can't believe he's gone. He was so young."

Something tells me Mrs. Hawkins believes her son's murder was connected to his gambling problem. "Mrs. Hawkins, did Austin have a bookie?"

She nods. "Austin owed him quite a bit of money, too."

The conversation I overheard in the restaurant replays in my mind. *Just a few more days, please. That's all I'm asking for.* Austin was on the phone with his bookie. I know it. Just like I know he was hoping to place more bets and win back the money he owed. But I don't feel like the case is as simple as he didn't have the money to pay off his debt and his bookie made him pay with his life instead. Something else was going on.

"Mrs. Hawkins, was Austin acting strangely at all over the past week?"

"Actually, yes. When he came home from work Friday night, he seemed nervous. He kept going to the front window and making sure no one was outside. I asked him if he was expecting anyone, but he said no."

So he was just as jumpy at home as he was at the restaurant. But was that connected to owing his bookie money? "Do you know his bookie's name?"

"No. When I brought it up, he'd just tell me I didn't know what I was talking about. I don't think he wanted me to know what he'd gotten himself into, but I did. He even stole a check from my checkbook once. I caught him with it, but he lied and said it must have fallen out of my checkbook because he'd found it on the floor." She starts sobbing all over again.

She seems convinced this is what caused her son's death, and the only way I'm going to find out if that's true or not is by coming clean about what I can do.

"Mrs. Hawkins, I should tell you the reason why I work with the Weltunkin PD so often."

She raises her head, and recognition flashes across her face. "Wait a second. I know who you are. You're that psychic lady."

That psychic lady. The way she says it tells me she doesn't believe in psychics. "I've helped solve a lot of cases, and I believe I can help you get closure regarding your son's death, but I'll need to see his room in order to do so."

She narrows her eyes at me. "Austin saw a psychic once. She told him about a sure thing. A bet he couldn't lose on." She scoffs. "That's the bet that got him into debt in the first place." She stands up. "I think it's time for you to leave."

So much for getting myself onto this case.

CHAPTER THREE

Mitchell meets me at Marcia's Nook at lunchtime. I've been here since Mrs. Hawkins kicked me out of her house hours ago. Thankfully, I bought a new mystery to occupy my time while I waited for Mitchell.

"Hey," he says, sliding into the seat across from me. "What do you have there?" He tilts the book toward me so he can read the cover. "You know, sometimes I think you purposely rented that office space so you'd be next door to a bookstore with a café."

"I'm not going to confirm or deny that," I say, placing my receipt in the book as a makeshift bookmark.

He laughs. "I'll take that as confirmation." He opens the pastry box in front of him, and his eyes widen. "Is this mocha coffee cake?"

"It is."

He grabs a fork and digs right in. With his mouth full,

he points his fork at the coffee cake and then me. Once he swallows, he says, "You're lucky you snatched me up before I proposed to Marcia. That woman knows how to bake."

"Don't let me stand in the way of your future 'Dad body.'"

He laughs. "How do you know that term? You don't watch TV, and you're not on social media."

"I told you. Just because I don't watch TV, doesn't mean I don't listen to it when you put it on." He watches it at my place just about every night.

He bobs his head and continues eating.

Marcia walks over with a big smile on her face. "Detective, long time no see."

He smiles up at her. "I was just telling Piper how she's lucky she admitted her feelings for me before I asked you to marry me."

Marcia dramatically snaps her fingers, swinging her arm in front of her. "Darn. I guess I lost out on that one." She winks at me before asking, "Do you need anything else? Coffee refill maybe?"

I finish the last sip of my third coffee of the day and say, "Yes, please!"

She shakes her head at me. "I can't believe you don't bleed coffee at this point."

"I haven't cut myself in a while, so I just might."

She keeps shaking her head as she walks away.

"How did it go with Mrs. Hawkins?" Mitchell asks.

It takes me all of sixty seconds to tell him about my short visit to her house.

"Yikes. I guess you're going to have to let Andrews take care of this case on his own."

"I'd feel better if I had even an iota of confidence he could solve it."

"He's actually not a bad cop when he isn't worried about you swooping in and solving his cases before he can."

I roll my eyes. "Yeah, and Officer Gilbert doesn't idolize and totally fangirl all over my dad." Officer Gilbert is a rookie on the force who happens to think my father was the greatest police detective of all time. He also happens to take my side over Officer Andrews's, so I feel a little bad for the "fangirl" comment.

Mitchell laughs. "I really do think Andrews will solve this one."

"I hope you're right because I'm not going to be able to sleep until I find out what happened to our waiter."

Mitchell reaches for my hand. "You have to stop blaming yourself. You can't save everyone from every bad thing that's going to happen."

"He's right," Marcia says, placing my coffee on the table. "Look at all the cases you've solved and the bad things you've prevented. Focus on those because if you dwell on the things you couldn't stop, you'll be miserable all your life."

"An incredible baker and she's brilliant," Mitchell says. "Seriously, Piper, you should watch out for this one."

"No one's buying it, Detective," Marcia says. "It's been obvious for a long time that you only have eyes for Piper."

He squeezes my hand. "Obvious to everyone but Piper, that is."

I was the last one to figure out Mitchell had feelings for me. That's just more proof that I don't always see what I'm supposed to. If I only knew how to fix that problem.

———

Tuesday morning, I still can't think of anything but Austin Hawkins. I feel like I failed him, so I spend my morning researching him, but that doesn't turn up much of anything helpful, and Mitchell is stuck working another case, which means I'm on my own. I grab my purse and go back to the restaurant, which is just opening for lunch.

"Table for one?" the hostess asks me.

"Yes, please." I decide it's best to act like a customer instead of announcing myself as a private investigator. I don't want word to get back to Mrs. Hawkins that I'm looking into her son's case after she threw me out of her house.

"Follow me." The hostess grabs a menu and brings me to a table that's nowhere near Austin's section from Friday night.

As I sit down, I ask, "Is Austin in today?"

"You know Austin?" she asks.

"Well, sort of. I've been here before, and he was my waiter. I was hoping to be seated in his section if he's working."

She looks down at the menu still in her hands. "He's not here, and he unfortunately won't be back."

"Oh?" I feign ignorance. "Did he quit?"

"No. He was actually murdered a couple days ago. It was in the paper, but I guess you didn't see it."

"How horrible. No, I didn't see it, but I admit I don't read the news much these days."

She hands me the menu. "Yeah, well, I can't blame you. It's depressing. Anyway, Cathy will be your server. She'll be with you shortly." She starts to walk away.

"I'm sorry for your loss," I call after her.

She stops and turns back to me. "I didn't really know him well, to be honest. It's just scary to think someone would shoot another person in their own car like that for no reason."

There's always a reason. And that's what I'm hoping to find out.

Cathy approaches my table a few minutes later. "Good afternoon. I'm Cathy, and I'll be your server today. Can I start you off with something to drink?"

"I'd love an unsweetened iced tea," I say.

"Sure thing. Do you know what you'd like to eat, or do you need a few more minutes to look over the menu?"

I haven't even glanced at it yet, but I immediately get an idea. "I was here the other night for dinner, and Austin —he was my waiter—recommended the lobster ravioli. It was fantastic." I make a show of scanning the menu. "Is there any chance you serve that for lunch as well?"

"Oh, um, no. It's not on the lunch menu, but I could ask the chef if he'd make it."

"That would be great. Thanks. Is Austin here? I'd love to thank him again for the recommendation. It was the best lobster ravioli I've ever had." I'm taking a huge risk asking for Austin again after the hostess already told me he was dead, but I need information and it's possible Austin talked to the other servers more than he talked to the hostess. I just hope the hostess and Cathy aren't too friendly and don't discuss my visit today.

"I guess you didn't hear." She looks down at the notepad in her hand. "Austin was killed over the weekend. It was tragic really."

"Oh, how horrible. I'm so sorry." I put my hand to my chest. "Were you two close?"

She shakes her head. "Not really. We talked some since we worked together, but Austin pretty much kept to himself. He usually had his air pods in so he could keep track of scores. He was big on sports. He watched games on his phone during his breaks. Got in trouble a couple times for doing that when he wasn't on break, too. But I shouldn't be telling you that. I don't mean to speak ill of the dead."

"No, of course not. He sounds like a real sports lover."

"He was. I think he was probably betting on some games, too. He was always eager for payday, you know?" She smiles. "I remember one night, he actually kissed his check and told me he was putting it down on a horse named Glory. I thought he was joking, but then I read in the paper about a horse that broke its leg in a race. Her name was Glory. She was supposed to be a sure thing. A lot of people lost money on that race, according to the reporter."

My senses tingle, and I know that's the sure bet the psychic told Austin about. The one that started his losing streak. I'm guessing the psychic was a fraud and told him to bet on the horse that was supposed to be a sure thing.

"It's a shame. You know they put horses down for things like that," she says. "Oh, listen to me rambling about a horse when you probably just want to eat. I'll ask the chef about your lobster ravioli for you."

"Thank you," I say. "Um, could you direct me to the restroom. I know I used it last time I was here, but for the life of me, I can't remember where it is." I hope she'll believe my lie because I need to make a speedy exit. Cathy's a talker, and I have a feeling she's going to bring up Austin's name to her coworkers. I don't want to be here when people ask her why she's bringing him up.

"It's back by the bar. You can't miss it."

"Thanks." I get up, grabbing my purse since I don't plan to come back. I'm surprised to see the bar is empty, but this isn't exactly the type of place people come on their lunch breaks. I'm really pushing my luck now, but I walk up to the bar and sit down.

"What can I get for you?" the bartender asks me. She's a pretty woman in her mid-thirties if I had to guess.

I'm not a drinker. Drinking and having visions don't mix well, so I say, "Ginger ale, please. I'm meeting someone, and I'm a little nervous. I'm hoping it will settle my stomach."

She nods and pours the drink.

"You might actually know the guy I'm meeting since he works here."

She slides the drink across the bar to me. "Oh yeah? What's his name?"

"Austin Hawkins. I met him the other night. He was my waiter, and we just sort of hit it off. He asked me out, and I suggested having drinks here since it's close to where I work." I'm rambling again. My nerves are completely shot since there are now three employees who can blow my cover.

The bartender tilts her head to the side. "I'm sorry to have to tell you this, but Austin passed away over the weekend."

I feign surprise. "Are you sure? I mean, I haven't spoken to him since Friday night, but I just can't believe he's..." I let the sentence trail off.

"Sorry, honey." She leans on the bar top. "If you ask me, you dodged a bullet. He was a shifty character.

Always talking on his phone in hushed whispers. I'm pretty good at reading people, and everything about him said he was into some things that he shouldn't have been."

"I see." I open my purse and pull out a five-dollar bill. "Thanks," I say, sliding the bill to her and walking out of the restaurant with my head down so the hostess can't make conversation with me.

It's not much, but I now know Austin Hawkins was involved in something that gave him a real reason to keep looking over his shoulder.

CHAPTER FOUR

"Mitchell, don't you look handsome this evening?" Mom says as she greets us for Ashwell family dinner night.

"Thank you, Mrs. Ashwell. You look lovely as always."

Mom blushes and ushers us inside. "Mitchell, you are going to have to start calling me Bonnie one of these days."

"As I told your husband, I just can't do it."

"Believe me, Mom, he's tried. It's more awkward than anything else," I say, patting Mitchell on the shoulder.

His face turns an adorable shade of red.

"Ah, hello, pumpkin," Dad says, pulling me in for a hug.

"Hi, Dad."

"Hello, Mr. Ashwell."

Dad shakes his head. "It's going to be really strange when you two are married one day and my son-in-law calls me Mr. Ashwell."

I hold up both hands. "Whoa. No one is getting married, so that's not a concern you should have, Dad." I'm pretty positive Mom and Dad have been planning our wedding from the second they found out we were dating. Maybe even before that. They are going to be in for a rude awakening when that day never comes. I've never seen myself as the type to say "I do."

"Dinner's on the table, so everyone into the dining room, please," Mom says.

I can't decide who's more uncomfortable by the topic of marriage, Mitchell or me. He looks green.

"Sorry about that," I say, taking a seat and putting my napkin in my lap.

"No problem. Your dad likes to try to give me gray hair. I'm used to it, though I expected a comment like that to come from your mom."

He and I both.

Mom's just starting to serve the food when the doorbell rings.

"Did you invite someone else to dinner?" I ask, my gaze volleying between Mom and Dad.

Dad shakes his head.

"I'll see who it is," Mom says, putting down the bowl of steamed broccoli.

"How was your weekend away?" Mitchell asks Dad, but before Dad can answer we hear someone say, "Sorry to intrude on family dinner night, but I need to speak with Piper right away. It's urgent."

Mitchell and I exchange a glance. I'm sure my expression is saying, *What is that lowlife Officer Andrews doing at my parents' house?*

Mitchell stands up, most likely to intercept Officer Andrews, but Mom's already led him into the dining room. "What are you doing here?" Mitchell practically growls.

Officer Andrews looks all too happy at Mitchell's disapproval. "Well, I know Tuesdays are family dinner night for the Ashwells, but seeing as how you came to my house on a previous case, I knew you'd be okay with me stopping by for this one."

Payback. That's what this is. Except the only reason why Mitchell and I stopped by his house was because Officer Andrews was keeping information from us that we needed for a case. I can't imagine why his case would bring him here, unless he heard about my visit to the restaurant today.

"Andrews, make it quick. Our dinner is getting cold," Dad says, and his tone makes it very clear that he will personally escort Officer Andrews from the house if need be.

"Sure thing, Tom," Officer Andrews says, and I can see the vein in Dad's forehead bulge. Only Dad's closest friends can call him Tom, and Officer Andrews is nowhere near Dad's friend. They're former colleagues who never got along, and Officer Andrews's hatred for me only makes their relationship worse.

"Piper, I have something for you," Officer Andrews says, and the smile on his face tells me I won't like this at all. He hands me a folded paper.

"What is it?" Mitchell asks, trying to intercept the paper, which I pull away from him. I don't care if he is my boyfriend. I'm not about to let him start fighting my battles for me.

"Go ahead," Officer Andrews says, read it aloud.

I want nothing more than to wipe that smug smile right off his face. I unfold the paper, which appears to be a printout of an email sent to me, and read it silently. Mitchell leans in to read it over my shoulder.

Ms. Ashwell,

My name is Austin Hawkins. I need your help. You see, I placed a rather large bet on some horses. I got a tip. I was told it was a sure thing. Don't ask me how the person who tipped me off knew. I'd rather not get into the details. But my bookie wasn't happy in the least to have to pay my winnings. I'm too afraid to put the money in the bank, so it's sitting in a suitcase in the trunk of my car. I know that's not a good hiding place, but I'm too afraid to leave it in my apartment.

I think someone is following me. I'm not sure if it's the bookie or someone he hired. Either way, I'm pretty sure this person is out to kill me and take the money back. I need you to find this person and stop them.

Austin

I don't know what to make of it. Is this why Austin

asked for more time? He knew he had a sure thing that would get him out of debt? More so, his winnings surpassed his debt and made him money if the bookie paid him. Was Mrs. Hawkins right about the bookie? Did he get upset with Austin and do something to him?

But none of that explains why I've never seen this email before when it was supposedly sent to me. I check the date of the email. It was sent on Sunday, the day Hawkins was killed. And then I notice something really strange. It's addressed to my personal email, not my work one. No one ever contacts me there because no one even knows the email address exists.

"It's a fake," I say. "I never received this."

Officer Andrews's smile widens. "Really? Then maybe you can explain this." He unfolds a second piece of paper and extends it to me.

My senses are tingling, so I already know what it's going to be, but I read it anyway.

Mr. Hawkins,

Let's meet up to discuss your case. I'll be at the Weltunkin Cemetery at eight tonight on the bench by Loretta Maywood's grave. It's on the north side of the cemetery. Go down the small hill to a group of four wooden benches.

Don't email me again. Just meet me there.

Piper

"Okay, first, I'd never sign a work email 'Piper.'" I

shake my head at Officer Andrews's lack of attention to detail. The email is clearly a fake. The part that's really concerning me is whoever did write this knows me well enough to mention my deceased grandmother by name and to know about my personal email address that I never use.

"You probably did that to throw us off."

"That's absurd," I say, tossing the paper onto my empty plate.

"As is this flimsy accusation," Mitchell adds. "You have no case against Piper. You're just wasting everyone's time."

"Flimsy?" Officer Andrews cocks his head. "Explain the email then."

"What's there to explain? Piper never emailed Hawkins. Someone hacked into her personal email account, probably knowing she never uses it, and answered Hawkins's emails."

"Likely story. Good luck convincing a jury of that."

I'm not even sure how Austin Hawkins got my personal email address to begin with. I opened it years ago and never once used it. Anyone looking to acquire my P.I. services would have gotten my work email from my website. Nothing about this is adding up.

"Besides, it's the perfect crime. Any good P.I. would see that. Hawkins claims his bookie is after him for the money. Piper kills the guy, and everyone suspects the bookie. We didn't find a suitcase of money in the trunk, so that was clearly taken by the one person Hawkins told it was there. The person who killed him for it. You." Officer Andrews crosses his arms and stares at me as if he's just figured out the entire case.

"If that were true, why would I hide the emails from you then?" I ask. "They clearly implicate the bookie."

Andrews lowers his arms. "You tell me, Ashwell. Maybe you thought you wouldn't be connected to the victim at all since you used your personal email to contact him. Maybe this was just a backup plan if we did uncover the communications."

"That's all conjecture," Mitchell says. "We both know you hate Piper, and you'd do anything to get back at her because you blame her for your suspension. It's not going to work, though, because she's innocent."

"Of course, you're going to say that," Officer Andrews says. "You're going to say whatever you need to come to your girlfriend's defense. That's why the chief is keeping you off this case, Brennan." He steps closer, getting right in Mitchell's face. "I'd be careful if I were you. She got me suspended, but she just might get you fired." He takes one step back and glares at me. "Or maybe she'll put you six feet under like Austin Hawkins."

Mitchell pulls his arm back, but I grab him before his fist can connect with Officer Andrews's face.

"Don't," I tell him. "He's not worth it."

"That's enough." Dad is on his feet. He's usually a

very calm person, but Officer Andrews committed the biggest offense in Dad's mind: he messed with me. "Andrews, you will leave now. You have no warrant, so you have no right to be here. If your vehicle isn't gone in the next sixty seconds, I'll file charges for trespassing and harassment. And if you don't think I'll be in Chief Johansen's office first thing in the morning to tell him exactly what I think about your junior detective work, then you're an even more incompetent cop than I ever realized."

Wow. The only other time I've seen Dad this worked up was when Mitchell got us into a car accident and Dad let him have it for almost killing me. Officer Andrews walks out without saying a word, although he does slam the front door behind him.

"Well," Mom says, "why don't we all sit down and try to enjoy dinner?" She hates any work talk at the dinner table, but after what just happened, I don't see how we can avoid it. Still, she picks up the bowl of steamed broccoli and passes it to Dad. "Broccoli, Thomas?"

"I need to close that email account," I say.

"No," Dad says. "If you do, it will only make you look guilty. Leave it be. They'll realize you never sent the email."

"Will they?" I ask. "Officer Andrews is the lead detective on the case. He isn't going to dig into this to see who really sent that email. He's content to blame me."

"I won't let him," Mitchell says.

"Neither will I," Dad says, nodding at Mitchell.

"Mitchell, let me get you a twice-baked potato." Mom holds out her hand for his plate, doing her best to steer the conversation to anything else.

"Thank you," he says, handing her his plate. Under the table, he reaches for my hand. The problem is it's my right hand, and I realize it before it's too late to stop the vision.

"I don't know if I can protect her when Andrews is clearly out for blood. At least not without it costing me my badge."

When my eyes open, everyone is staring at me.

"Did you just read me?" Mitchell asks, removing his hand from mine.

I promised I'd never read him against his will again, but I didn't mean to. "It wasn't intentional. You grabbed my right hand."

"Oh. I didn't realize." He stands up. "Would you excuse me for a minute?" He walks toward the bathroom in the hallway, and I follow.

"Mitchell."

He stops and faces me. "What did you see?"

"That you're willing to lose your badge to protect me, but I'm not going to let you do that."

He rakes a hand through his hair. "I don't want to fight with you about this, so could we not make this into an argument? I think when you read my thoughts like that, I should get a free pass or something since you weren't supposed to know them."

I get what he's saying, but it's not like I can just pretend I didn't have the vision. Being in a relationship is turning out to be a lot harder than I thought it would be.

CHAPTER FIVE

The rest of Ashwell family dinner night was virtually silent, except for Mom talking about things like the weather and Max's recent vet visit, where the vet complimented Max's improved temperament. She gave Jezebel credit for that since Jez has been teaching Max how a dog is supposed to behave. Mitchell dropped me off afterward and went straight home. Apparently, agreeing not to argue means not talking at all, so I'm not sure how today will go if Mitchell shows up at the office.

Dad isn't here, which means he's at the station talking to Chief Johansen as promised. I'm not surprised in the least. Dad doesn't make empty threats. I also have no doubt Mitchell is with him, pleading my case and probably trying to get on this investigation to put an end to Officer Andrews's false accusations. It would make sense for Mitchell to take over the case. Officer Andrews should never have gotten it in the first place.

The wait is killing me, and the coffees I got us all from Marcia's Nook are getting colder by the minute. I eat my chocolate chip scone and half of Mitchell's before they both show up.

"Hey," Mitchell says, his voice full of sympathy until his gaze lands on the food. "Did you eat half of my scone?"

I shrug. "Don't be so late next time."

Dad laughs and quickly grabs the last scone before I can dig into that one, too. He sits down and removes his coffee from the drink caddy. "We have news."

Mitchell sits across from me, but instead of eating the rest of the scone, he motions that I can finish it.

I shake my head. "I was only eating to pass the time. I'm not even hungry."

"Nice. This is why most people have social media, by the way. It's great for killing time in moments like this and ensures your boyfriend actually gets to eat his breakfast."

"Piper's not most people," Dad says, winking at me.

"Very true," Mitchell says, his tone softening.

"Lay it on me already, you two. What happened?"

Mitchell reaches for his coffee. "Officer Andrews has requested me to be his partner on this investigation."

"Why would he do that?" I ask, but before Mitchell can respond, the truth slams into me like a Mack truck. "Because he thinks I'm guilty and he wants you to be there when he arrests me for murder."

Mitchell's grip on his to-go cup tightens and coffee spills all over my desk. I jump up to avoid getting soaked. "Sorry," he says, tossing the cup in the garbage before grabbing napkins and soaking up the liquid. "You are not getting arrested, though. We all know those emails are bogus. You didn't send them, so you are not going to jail for this. Even Andrews knows he doesn't have enough to pin this on you."

"Then why did he request you as his partner?" I ask.

"Most likely to avoid being pulled from the case all together," Dad says. "Though that still might happen. It depends on how well he gets along with you."

"With *me*?" I ask.

"Chief Johansen wants you on the case as well. He's giving you the opportunity to prove your innocence," Dad says.

I smirk. "Let me guess. That was your idea."

Dad smiles. "It didn't take much to convince him. You've made him a true believer, pumpkin."

But this also means I have to work with Officer Andrews. I can't say I'm happy about that. And Mrs. Hawkins doesn't want me in her home, which will make reading anything that belonged to Austin very difficult. Then there's the issue of me not being able to step foot inside the restaurant where Austin worked after I conned three employees yesterday, so I'd have to find a way out of that if the case takes us back there.

Mitchell finishes cleaning up the coffee, tossing a big

pile of napkins into the trash can. "My guess is Andrews will pull himself off the case in no time."

It's a toss-up which one of us hates the other more. I'm not taking myself off the case, though, so if one of us leaves, it will be him.

"What's our first step?" I ask.

"I suggest we go to the station to talk to Andrews and find out everything he's uncovered so far," Mitchell says. "The only other alternative is bringing him here, which I doubt you want to do."

"No way. At the station, he has to at least be civil since the chief is there," I say.

"My thoughts exactly." Mitchell's on his feet already, so I stand up. "Dad, are you coming?"

"Do you really think I'd let my baby girl go into the lion's den without me?"

"One, I'm not a baby by any means. And two, I'm not afraid of Officer Andrews."

"You'll always be my baby, but I know you're not afraid of him. I just want to make it clear he's not intimidating any one of us." Dad directs the last statement at Mitchell. Out of the three of us, he's the one who's most likely to react in a heated moment. He needs to keep his cool so we can show up Officer Andrews the right way.

Mitchell nods to both of us. "You lead. I'll follow."

Dad walks around his oversized desk—still a sore subject since this was my P.I. agency and he bought a desk that dwarfs mine—and claps Mitchell on the shoulder. "Good man. You can drive, too."

"No way," I say. "I'm not sitting in the back of Mitchell's patrol car. Officer Andrews would love that way too much."

"Okay, I'll drive," Dad says.

"I need to run into Marcia's Nook first. I lost my entire breakfast somehow," Mitchell says.

———

Officer Andrews glares at us the second we enter the police station. I expected no less, but I keep a straight face and head right for his desk.

"Hey, Piper. Nice to see you here," Officer Wallace says.

"Thanks. Nice to see you, too. How's Harry doing?" Harry is Officer Wallace's K9 partner.

"He's good. We just wrapped up a case. Drug bust."

"Congrats to you both, then."

"Thanks. I'll pass them along to Harry," he says with a smile.

Officer Andrews rolls his eyes. He really doesn't like anyone at the station, but he hates anyone who likes me.

"Good morning, partner," I say with as much fake sweetness as I can manage as I sit down at his desk. "We're ready to dive right in, so tell us what you've got."

Officer Andrews smirks, adjusts his tie, and sits down.

"Okay, the prime suspect is a psychic P.I. by the name of Piper Ashwell."

"Enough," Mitchell says. "Give us hard facts and nothing else before I have you removed from this case."

"Planning to go tell on me, Brennan?" Officer Andrews snaps.

"Is there a problem?" Chief Johansen says in a stern voice behind me.

"I'm just getting these three up to speed with the details of the case. Right now, all my evidence points to her." Officer Andrews points the file folder at me.

"Your evidence?" I ask. "You mean two emails, which I've already told you I never received or sent? You do realize anyone can send an email and make it look like it's from anyone they want, don't you? You just type in a known email address in the sender field. I can show you how right now if you'd like."

"How do you explain the fact that Austin Hawkins was lured to your grandmother's burial site?" Officer Andrews asks.

"I can't because I don't know who sent it. However, as you've just proven, a simple internet search connects me to Loretta Maywood. I'm sure whoever sent the email found that out the same way you did, Officer Andrews."

Chief Johansen crosses his arms. "I suggest the four of you get out there and find some real evidence that leads to a killer. And if I hear anymore bickering from the group, *someone* will be removed from the case." He's intentionally being vague about who that someone will be so we all feel threatened.

I stand up. "Let's go."

"Good idea," Dad says.

"And where exactly are you proposing we go?" Officer Andrews asks.

"Austin Hawkins's house, of course. I need to read some of his belongings."

Officer Andrews throws up his hands. "Great. So we're going to count on the spirits to guide us in this case. This should be very helpful."

"Problem, Andrews?" Chief Johansen asks.

Officer Andrews jumps, as if he forgot the chief is standing here. He shakes his head. "No, sir."

"Good. Happy to hear it. Oh, and Ashwell?"

Dad and I both look in the chief's direction.

His gaze volleys between us, and he realizes his mistake. "Piper, that is. I need concrete evidence. I can't convict anyone based on a sense you get, understood?"

"Understood, Chief."

Officer Andrews walks past us. "I'm driving separately. Meet you there."

We walk out to Dad's car, and I watch Officer Andrews peel out of the parking lot as if he's involved in a high-speed car chase instead of simply on his way to interview the victim's mother.

"He's like a dog marking his territory all over this case," I say.

"Except dogs are much smarter than he is," Mitchell says.

"No argument there."

Officer Andrews beats us to Austin Hawkins's house. Big surprise. We park behind him so he can't leave until we let him out. It's a small victory, but I'll take it. Mrs. Hawkins is just opening the door for him when we walk up the front steps. Her eyes land on me, and I can tell she's about to protest my being here, so I walk right up to her and say, "I'm so sorry someone posing as a psychic set your son on the wrong path. I hope you'll let me try to rectify things and show you how a *real* psychic can help."

Dad puts his arm around my shoulder. "My daughter is the best in the business. If anyone can find out who did this to your son, it's Piper."

Officer Andrews clearly wants to say something, but he's refraining. Most likely because he'll get nowhere if Mrs. Hawkins won't let us inside.

"Mrs. Hawkins, please allow me to show you what I can do, and if you're still uncomfortable with my involvement in the case, I'll leave," I say.

"I'd take her up on that offer," Officer Andrews says, clearly believing I'll fail.

Mrs. Hawkins considers it for a moment before nodding and allowing us to come inside.

"If you would show me to Austin's room, I can get started. I'm sure you have a lot to do, so I'll try to be as quick as possible."

She motions up the stairs before leading the way. I follow, noting all the pictures of Austin from birth to graduation.

"Your son is your only child," I say.

"Clearly," Officer Andrews mumbles behind me on the stairs. "Anyone can see that."

"He is," Mrs. Hawkins says. She turns left at the top of the stairs. "That's his room there."

The door is closed, and I get the sense she doesn't want to go inside the room. "May I?" I ask.

She nods and stays where she is.

"Perhaps Officer Andrews, you, and I should talk in the living room while Detective Brennan and Piper look in Austin's room," Dad suggests.

Mrs. Hawkins nods again and starts down the stairs.

"The poor woman looks like she's going to fall apart," Mitchell says once we're alone.

"I can't blame her." I reach for the doorknob and open the door. The room is small and still decorated like a teenage boy lives in it. There's a twin bed against one wall, a dresser and desk along another wall, and a bean bag chair in the corner.

"I haven't sat in a bean bag chair in years," Mitchell says, flopping down into the brown pleather chair.

I try to ignore him and focus on the energy in the room. There's a lot of tension, like Austin was constantly on edge. I walk over to the desk where there's a schedule of upcoming sporting events. Some are circled in red. "I guess these were bets he placed," I say.

Mitchell grunts, and the sound of Styrofoam beading on pleather alerts me he's struggling to get out of the bean bag chair. "These things are comfy but really hard to get out of once you sink into them."

I pick up the schedule in my right hand and close my eyes.

"This is the last one before I pay what I owe. I promise. I'm good for it."

The vision ends just as quickly as it began. Something still feels off to me about the bookie being the one behind Austin's death, but if he's not, why did I see it in my vision? I don't see things unless they're important to the case I'm working on. So, what am I missing?

Mitchell's at my side now. "Anything?"

"Nothing we didn't already know. I can't piece together why the bet was so important."

"It was mentioned in the email he sent you," Mitchell says. "And we know you didn't respond to Austin's email, so that could mean it was the killer who did. He might be trying to pin this on you for some reason."

Bingo! My entire body tenses as my senses confirm what Mitchell just said. "That's it. Whoever killed Austin Hawkins wants me to go to jail for the murder."

"Of course, you'd try to spin this case in that direction," Officer Andrews says from the doorway because he apparently couldn't stay downstairs. "I saw that coming a mile away. Maybe I'm psychic, too." He scoffs.

Mitchell advances on Officer Andrews. "Let's get something straight. Piper had nothing to do with this guy's murder. If you're going to be biased in this investigation, I'll go over your head to Chief Johansen. You've already been suspended once. It can easily happen again. Though I doubt you'd get your badge back this time."

Officer Andrews's fists clench at his sides, and for a moment, I think he's going to take a swing at Mitchell. But then he smiles and looks past Mitchell at me. "I'm going to enjoy putting you in handcuffs." He turns and walks out.

Mitchell looks like he's going to charge after Officer Andrews, but I hold him back. "Don't. Just let him go. I need to find something in this room to give us a lead, or he really will find a reason to put me in handcuffs." We don't have time for a display of masculine rivalry right now, even if Mitchell is trying to defend me. I need him focused so he can help me.

"I'm not sure I've ever hated a colleague as much as I hate that man. He doesn't deserve to wear a badge."

I step toward him. "I need you to help me right now, but you can't do that if you're worked up over Officer Andrews's empty threats. So tell me; can I count on you to help me search this room, or do I have to do this on my own?" It's a low move considering I know Mitchell always has my back, but I don't have time to coddle his male ego right now. We need to find this killer. Especially since we don't know if Austin's death is an isolated event or if the murderer is just getting started.

"Whatever you need," Mitchell says, giving me a nod.

"Good. You search the dresser drawers while I check out the desk."

"Piper," Dad says from the doorway.

I'm never going to get anywhere if people keep interrupting me. I try not to show my annoyance as I turn to face him. "Yeah?"

"I just found out something I think you might want to know."

The way he said "found out" makes my senses tingle. "Let me guess. Officer Andrews was withholding information."

Dad nods. "When Austin was found in his car, there was a handheld mirror on the passenger seat."

"Why is that important?" Mitchell asks, his gaze volleying between us.

I smile for the first time on this case. "Because it's something I can read." Before I can get too excited Mrs. Hawkins appears in the hallway behind Dad.

"I want you out of my house, and I don't want you to ever come back here. How dare you?" she yells at me.

"I'm sorry, but I don't understand why you're so upset," I say. And then I see Officer Andrews's smiling face behind her.

"I don't understand why any of you would bring the

prime suspect for my son's murder into my home. What kind of police department does something like that?"

Mitchell holds up a hand to stop her. "Mrs. Hawkins—"

Her entire body shakes as she lunges forward and grabs me by both arms. "I hope you rot in a jail cell for the rest of your life!"

CHAPTER SIX

Her grief and anger overwhelm me, and the next thing I know, I'm in Mitchell's arms and he's carrying me out of the house. He gets me into the back seat of Dad's BMW and sits beside me.

"Are you okay, Piper?"

Rage courses through me when I see Officer Andrews exit the house. I reach for my seat belt, which Mitchell just clicked into place, but before I can get anywhere, he's holding me back.

"Piper, relax. You're channeling some serious rage right now. Don't do anything you're going to regret later. No matter how much you hate him and how much he deserves a punch in the face, you can't assault a police officer and get away with it. Especially not when that police officer is already out for your blood."

"He did that on purpose. He's trying to stop me from

solving this case so he can have the pleasure of putting me in handcuffs."

"I completely agree with you, and that's why I'm going to let the chief know all about this stunt he pulled. Don't worry. But you have to let me handle him the right way."

"How are you so calm right now?" I ask, forcing my gaze off Officer Andrews and onto Mitchell.

"I'm not. Believe me it's taking every ounce of self-control to stay in this vehicle with you and not beat the crap out of him. But I know if I do that, I'll be hurting you because I'll be thrown off this case, and you need me right now." He cups my cheek. "Please try to calm down." He takes several deep breaths, trying to get me to do the same. It's a trick he learned from my father on the very first case we ever worked together.

I give in and mimic his breathing.

"Better?" he asks.

"Being an empath sucks," I say.

He chuckles and leans his forehead against mine.

"I know what you're doing. You're trying to distract me with your own emotions."

"Is it working?" He pulls back and smiles at me.

"A little. Thanks." I twist the ring on my left pinky.

"Good." Mitchell looks out the window. "Now where is your father?"

Since we're blocking Officer Andrews in the driveway, no one can leave until my dad shows up. "He's most likely still inside the house, trying to repair the damage Officer Andrews did and calming down Mrs. Hawkins."

Mitchell nods. "If anyone can, it's your dad."

That's true. Dad is a people person. It's one of the reasons why he is such a great detective. Everyone loves him—other than the people he's put behind bars, of course.

He finally comes out of the house a few minutes later. When he gets into the car, he turns to look at Mitchell and me. He doesn't ask if everything is okay. He can see I'm calmer, and he knows Mitchell is responsible for that. "We're off to the morgue so you can read that handheld mirror."

We stop for some sandwiches on the way and eat in the car. Most of my meals are on-the-go these days. I'm not even hungry, but I force myself to eat two-thirds of my Italian sub. Mitchell calls Chief Johansen to let him know about the stunt Officer Andrews pulled, and even though the phone isn't on speaker, I can hear the chief's choice words with no problem at all.

"Well, I'd say Andrews is in for a fun conversation with the chief," Mitchell says after he hangs up.

"Johansen won't put up with pettiness," Dad says, pulling into a parking spot. "I don't doubt Andrews will be off this case by the time we're finished here."

That would be nice, but I'm not so sure. If the chief has any doubts about me at all, he might want someone other than Mitchell working the case. Officer Andrews is the only one at the station who outwardly rejects my psychic abilities. The only time he was ever nice to me was when I used my abilities to read his wife and find out she wasn't having an affair. He conveniently forgot all about that very soon after and actually despises me even more now.

We can speculate until we're blue in the face, but I'd rather do something more productive, like clear my own name in this case. I get out of the vehicle and head into the morgue. Reading dead bodies is something I try to avoid doing at all costs, and I'm thankful that I don't have to resort to that. At least not just yet.

Dad walks up to the mortician. "Rudy, nice to see you. Piper, this is Rudy. Mitchell, I believe you two already know each other."

Mitchell nods, and Rudy returns it.

Rudy is in his fifties with a gray beard and not a single hair on his head. He extends his hand to me, but then retracts it when I don't take it. "That's right. You don't do the whole handshaking thing," he says to me.

"Only if I'm trying to read someone."

"I appreciate you not reading me." He gives a nervous chuckle, making me wonder what skeletons are residing in his closet. He turns around and picks up an evidence bag on the counter. "I believe this is what you're here for. It's already been dusted for fingerprints. I think CSI found multiple prints. I haven't heard if they've gotten the results yet."

"Multiple prints as in different sets?" Mitchell says. "So they might have the killer's prints?"

"I'm not sure, but it's possible," Rudy says. "From what I hear, Piper will be able to tell us if the killer touched this mirror long before the fingerprint results come in."

"If he did, I should be able to pick up on his energy as well as Austin Hawkins's," I say, taking the evidence bag. I carefully open it and reach for the mirror with my left hand. "I have this same mirror in my bathroom at home. I don't think I've ever used it, though. I believe it comes in a set with some other grooming supplies, if I'm remembering correctly."

"There's nothing fancy about it, so I don't doubt it's a typical mirror sold with a set," Rudy says.

I transfer the mirror to my right hand.

Austin's image fills the reflective surface of the mirror, but then he tilts it to see behind him down the street. His pulse quickens, and he switches the mirror to his other side to do the same thing.

I open my eyes and switch the mirror to my left hand again. "He was using this to see if anyone was following him," I say. "I couldn't quite tell where he was, but he was looking back at the road behind him, making sure he didn't have a tail."

Rudy laughs. "I know you mean a person following him, but the way you said it made me picture Austin with an animal tail."

Mitchell snickers. What is it about men acting like little boys? I roll my eyes.

"Can you sense the killer's energy, Piper?" Dad asks.

"Let me try to focus on that." I place the mirror back in my right hand.

"I'll never use this thing," I say, tossing the mirror in the bottom drawer of my vanity.

My eyes snap open, and I drop the mirror. It falls to the floor, and the glass shatters into several pieces at my feet.

"Piper." Mitchell takes me by both arms and turns me toward him. "What is it? Did you see the killer?"

"No. I..." I can't say it aloud because I don't see how it could be possible.

Rudy bends down to pick up the mirror and broken glass. "CSI is not going to be happy about this."

"I'll explain, Rudy," Dad says before turning to me. "Pumpkin, do you know who the second set of prints belong to?"

I nod and swallow the lump in my throat. "They're mine."

Someone claps from the doorway, and we all turn to see Officer Andrews. "Oh, my day just keeps getting better and better."

"What the hell are you doing here?" Mitchell asks him.

"My job."

"I'm surprised you still have one after the conversation I had with Chief Johansen."

Officer Andrews nods. "I did get a call from him saying I need to report for a meeting in an hour, but I thought I'd follow you three and see what you were up to first. I'm glad I did because I think the chief will be singing a different tune when I tell him Piper just implicated herself."

"She did no such thing," Dad says.

Everyone is talking at once, and I can't take it. I need to get out of here before I completely lose it. I push past Mitchell and Officer Andrews and step outside, tilting my head up and letting the sun warm my face. Footsteps behind me alert me to Mitchell's presence before he speaks.

"We'll figure this out," he says. "We'll go to your place, find your mirror, and then show everyone that you only saw yourself in that vision because you own the same mirror. That's all. Besides, I'm sure the fingerprints the CSI team lifted off the mirror are going to match Austin's and the killer's, which will clear you immediately."

"We'll see about that," Officer Andrews says, walking outside.

Mitchell whirls around on him. "Don't you have a meeting to go to?"

"I think the chief will understand why I'm late when I bring him a key piece of evidence."

"You're delusional if you think this is going to play out

the way you want it to," Mitchell says, positioning himself between Officer Andrews and me.

"You sound scared, Brennan. Is it possible you're starting to doubt your girlfriend's innocence in all this?"

Dad clamps a hand down on Officer Andrews's shoulder. "I'd watch what you imply about my daughter, Andrews. Or did you forget the law states 'innocent until proven guilty'?"

Officer Andrews shrugs off Dad's hand. "She's going to prove herself guilty, and I'm going to be there to see it."

"No, you're not," Mitchell says.

"She has to produce her mirror. Even you must know that, Brennan." Officer Andrews crosses his arms. "So what are we all waiting for?"

"What do you mean *we?*" Mitchell asks through clenched teeth.

"I'm coming with you."

"You are not welcome inside my apartment," I say, moving to the side of Mitchell so I can face Officer Andrews head-on.

He lowers his arms. "Fine. I'll stay in the doorway, and you can bring the mirror to me. Or more likely you won't be able to bring it to me since it was your mirror found in Austin Hawkins's car, proving you were in contact with him."

I want nothing more than to see the look on his face when I find my mirror exactly where I left it in my apartment. "Let's go then."

"Is that an invite?" Officer Andrews asks in a mocking tone.

"The one and only invite you'll ever get," I say, turning on my heel and heading for Dad's BMW.

"Piper, are you sure about this?" Mitchell asks, catching up with me.

"Can you think of a better way to get him off my back?" I open the front passenger door and meet Mitchell's gaze.

"What if...?" He turns and looks over his shoulder at Officer Andrews, who is getting into his patrol car.

"What? You don't believe me now?"

"No. Of course, I know you had nothing to do with all of this. It's just that..." He looks down at his feet.

I shut the car door and stand directly in front of him. "Mitchell, what aren't you saying?"

Dad is behind me now, listening in.

He meets my gaze, and his eyes are full of remorse. "I threw that mirror out the other day. I was cleaning out a drawer in your vanity so I could keep a few items at your place. I mean I'm there so much. I've never seen you use a handheld mirror, and the only other things in that drawer were some old batteries and a travel-size toothpaste that had expired two years ago, so I figured you never used any of the stuff."

Dad curses under his breath.

I'm stunned. Not because Mitchell made himself completely at home in my apartment—he's done that ever since we met. I'm stunned because Mitchell just helped make a case against me.

"I'm sorry. I never thought something like this would happen," Mitchell says.

"Everyone is going to think that mirror really belonged to Piper now." Dad swings his arm out in my direction, unable to conceal his anger.

"Because it did," I say, knowing it's true. "It was my mirror. CSI will find my fingerprints and Mitchell's. And Officer Andrews will have even more evidence against me."

CHAPTER SEVEN

Officer Andrews's patrol car pulls up alongside us. He lowers the window and says, "What's the holdup?"

Without saying a word, I get into the car. Dad and Mitchell follow suit, and Dad starts the engine before asking, "What now? If we go to your apartment, we aren't going to find that mirror."

"I know that, but I need time to think," I say.

Dad pulls out of the parking spot and heads for my apartment.

"Mitchell, play the game," I say. The game is something we use often on cases. I clear my mind, and Mitchell or Dad starts asking me easy questions I know the answers to. Once I'm in a meditative state, they throw in questions pertaining to the case we're working on, and the answers just come to me. I don't usually get too many answers because one will inevitably shock me out of the meditative state and put an end to the game, but it's still very useful.

"What am I supposed to ask you about?" He leans forward so his head is between the two front seats.

"I don't know. How the killer knows me? Why he's trying to frame me for murder? You figure it out." I rub my forehead with my thumb and index finger.

"Pumpkin, you need to try to calm down, or the game isn't going to work at all," Dad says, eyeing me briefly before turning his attention back to the road.

Calm down? Sure. I'm being implicated in a murder investigation. What's there not to be calm about?

I lean my head back on the headrest and take several deep, cleansing breaths. My heart rate is through the roof, though. I can't calm myself. "This isn't working. I know he's behind us, smiling the entire way to my place because he knows he's going to win. He's going to get to cuff me and haul me into the station." My fists are clenched in my lap.

Mitchell reaches forward and places his hand on my arm. "I'm not letting that happen. He's not going to lay a finger on you, or he's a dead man."

I turn my tear-filled eyes toward him. "If you lose your badge because of me, I'll never forgive you. I don't want you jeopardizing your career over me. Do you understand?"

"Piper, you can't ask me to sit back and do nothing

while he tries to spin a case against you. No way. I won't do that." He leans back in his seat.

"I'm not letting you put our relationship before being a cop, Mitchell."

He sits forward again. "Even if we weren't dating, I'd still react this way. You're my partner. Any cop on the force would put their partner first. It's what we do."

"He's right, pumpkin. And besides, I'm not on the force anymore. I *will* come between you and anyone who tries to put you in handcuffs."

I really couldn't ask for better men in my life, but even knowing what lengths they'd both go to for me, they won't be able to stop Officer Andrews. He's going to have enough evidence against me to at least haul me down to the station for questioning.

I'm not really sure why we're going to my apartment at this point. I'm not going to find the mirror or anything else that can help me. I know no one got into my apartment. Jezebel would never allow that to happen, and even if someone did manage to get past her, I would have read that kind of distress off of her. It means someone took my garbage and rifled through it. But then why give the mirror to Austin in the first place. It doesn't make sense that the killer would give Austin a mirror that he could use to keep an eye out for the killer. Just thinking about it is giving me a major headache.

When we pull up to my apartment complex, I take a deep breath, trying to formulate a plan. Nothing comes to me. This is a wild goose chase, and we all know it. Even Officer Andrews.

"I feel sick," I tell Mitchell as we get out of the car and head for the front door of the building.

He runs his hand up and down on my back. "So do I. We'll figure something out, though. The three of us have to be able to fool Andrews if we put our heads together."

We walk inside, and I do my best to ignore the smile plastered on Officer Andrews's face. The elevator ride feels excruciatingly long since the only sound is Officer Andrews humming the music that accompanies final Jeopardy. I know he's just trying to unnerve me, but it's totally working.

When we finally get to my apartment, I open the door, and Jez greets me with a happy little yip and a big wag of her tail. She's just as happy to see Mitchell and Dad, but when Officer Andrews steps into the doorway, Jez does something I've never seen her do. She growls. I'm talking full-on snarling.

"Easy, Jez," I say, bending down and stroking the top of her head.

"Friendly dog," Officer Andrews says, but he doesn't dare step foot into the apartment.

"Dogs are great judges of character," I say. "She knows a bad man when she sees him, don't you, Jez?"

She growls at Officer Andrews again.

"That's my smart girl. You stay here and watch the

bad man while Mommy, Mitchell, and Grandpa go into the other room."

"You know dogs can't understand all that," Officer Andrews says.

"Oh, really?" I stand up and put my hands on my hips. "Jez, if the bad man steps into the apartment, you have my permission to bite him in his man parts."

Mitchell laughs. "She'll totally do it, and since you'd be trespassing—seeing as how Piper told you that you aren't welcome, and you have no warrant to force entry—Jezebel is well within her rights to protect her home and her owner. I wouldn't move if I were you."

To his credit, Officer Andrews is smart enough to look scared. I pat Jez's head again before retreating to the bathroom. Once we're all inside, Mitchell closes the door.

Even though I know the mirror isn't there, I open the bottom drawer of the vanity. Sure enough, there's a toothbrush, toothpaste, comb, aftershave, and a razor. "Seriously, Mitchell? How did you think it was okay to move things into my apartment without asking me first?"

"I do have my own key," he says.

"Which I didn't give you, did I?" I glare at Dad.

"You know this is not what I had in mind when I made you a key to Piper's place," Dad says.

"Yes, but that was also before we started dating."

I gesture back and forth between Mitchell and me. "We don't live together. I don't do the whole cohabitating thing."

"I've slept on your couch multiple times. I like to brush my teeth and occasionally shower."

Dad holds up a hand to stop us. "Okay, this isn't the time for that conversation. Though it's definitely a conversation you two should have in the near future. We have no mirror to produce, so what's our next step?"

"I think we have to go to Chief Johansen before Andrews does," Mitchell says.

"Go to him with what?" I ask. "I highly doubt my winning personality is going to sway him when there's actual evidence linking me to a crime."

Mitchell takes my left hand in his. "Andrews thinks he has the upper hand right now. Our best move is to take it from him by beating him to the punch. If we go to the chief and tell him what happened, he'll be more likely to believe us than Andrews."

I'm not so sure that's true. The chief is all about tangible evidence, and we have none. Still, there's nothing else to do, so I open the bathroom door and walk back into the kitchen where Jez is sitting with her eyes and pretty white teeth trained on Officer Andrews.

"Well?" he asks, making the mistake of raising his hands in the air, which prompts a whole lot of growling from Jez. He steps back into the hallway. "Easy. I'm not coming in."

"Good girl, Jez," I say.

"You two go on ahead. I'll hitch a ride with Officer Andrews after I walk Jezebel," Dad says.

"What? I'm not waiting here while you walk the dog." Officer Andrews starts down the hall, and Jez follows him. "What is she doing?" he asks me.

"She understood everything my dad said, so I suggest you go with my father to walk Jez before she gets upset." I know Dad is stalling so Mitchell and I can talk to Chief Johansen without Officer Andrews present, and I love him even more for it. I give a small wave and smile. "Be good for Grandpa, Jez, and keep an eye on the bad man." I point to Officer Andrews before turning for the elevator.

"What about the mirror?" Officer Andrews calls after us, but we're already inside the elevator.

I close the doors and let out a deep sigh. "This case might be the death of me."

"I won't let that happen." Mitchell presses his shoulder up against mine.

"You keep saying that, but this time, things might be out of your control."

———

I should have known Officer Andrews would call the chief after we stranded him at my apartment. Chief Johansen is expecting Mitchell and me, and he's already well aware of the evidence against me.

"Ashwell, my office," he says the second we step into the station. "Brennan, you stay put."

I'm not surprised he wants to talk to me alone.

Mitchell isn't the least bit happy about it, but I place my hand on his forearm. "It's fine. I'll be okay."

His shoulders don't relax any, but he allows me to go into the office on my own.

"Have a seat," Chief Johansen says, taking his own seat behind his desk. He's a tall man, so even seated, his form is intimidating.

"Thank you," I say, even though I'm not sure what I'm thanking him for since I'm pretty positive I'm about to get a stern lecture that may or may not result in my arrest.

"First, I want you to understand that the fact that this conversation is happening here in my office and not in an interrogation room is because I'm extending you a courtesy seeing as you've helped us solve many cases in the past."

"I understand." I fold my hands in my lap, trying to appear much calmer than I feel.

"Good. Now, can you explain the fingerprints on the mirror?" Chief Johansen asks.

"Yes. Detective Brennan informed me that he disposed of my mirror a few days ago. It must have somehow come into Austin Hawkins's possession after that."

"I'm well aware of your relationship with Detective Brennan, but what proof do you have that the mirror was thrown away other than Mitchell's word?"

"Are you saying the word of one of your police detectives isn't good enough?" I ask.

"Ashwell, I'm going to level with you. If you two weren't involved, it might be, but given the circumstances, I need some real proof. Andrews is working a pretty solid case against you with the emails and the fingerprints on the mirror. You're going to have to give me something to combat that with, or I'm not going to be able to help you."

"Unless someone went through my garbage and saw —" I stop mid-sentence. "That's it. Someone went through my garbage."

"Is that what your senses are telling you?" he asks.

"Yes."

"Great. Then who was it?"

Of course, he'd ask that. "Chief, if I knew that, I'd have the case solved already." Knowing who took the mirror out of my garbage would most likely mean knowing the identity of the killer.

"Then I guess you and Brennan need to do some detective work. Speak to the garbage disposal crew. Find out who had access to your trash." He picks up his pen and taps the point against the blotter on the desktop. "Do I really need to tell you how to do your job?"

"No, sir. That is if I'm free to go and prove my innocence."

"You are. For now."

I stand up.

"But, Ashwell, if Andrews comes up with any more evidence against you, that's going to change, so I suggest you work quickly."

CHAPTER EIGHT

"I wish I'd been in that office when the chief told Andrews he couldn't arrest you on murder charges." Mitchell forks the last bite of his strawberry cheesecake into his mouth. He ordered it with our dinner to celebrate the fact that I'm still a free woman. For the time being.

"You're not off the hook, you know. I'm in this mess because of you." I point my fork in his direction.

He places his empty plate on the coffee table. "I know. I'm sorry I didn't talk to you about the drawer. I just thought you'd handle it better if we didn't have a conversation beforehand."

I don't like talking about feelings. I think it stems from my grandmother being an empath and getting some of those empathic abilities myself. I deal with other people's emotions when I read them. At the end of the day, I don't want to talk about feelings. "I get it, and I know it's not your fault someone went through my trash."

"Your dad set up a meeting first thing tomorrow morning with the garbage crew. We'll get to the bottom of this." He sounds so sure, but I'm guessing he's trying to convince himself as much as me.

I stretch my arms over my head. "I'm beat. Are you sleeping on the couch, or are you actually heading home?"

"Normally, I'd say the couch, but given the whole 'we don't live together' conversation from earlier, I think I'll go home." He stands up, which makes Jez pick her head up from my lap. "You two go to bed. You both look beat."

"Such a flatterer," I say with a yawn.

"You're only proving my point." Mitchell leans down and kisses the top of Jezebel's head and then the top of mine. "Goodnight, my beautiful girls."

"Mitchell, thanks for wanting to take a swing at Andrews today. I appreciate what you were willing to do for me."

"Your dad and I have your back, Piper. You're not going down for this. I promise." As much as I know he can't really keep me out of jail if Andrews manages to find more evidence against me, I know he'll do everything in his power to try.

"Goodnight, Mitchell."

———

My office door opens, and to my surprise it's Marcia who walks in carrying a white pastry bag and a drink caddy with three coffees.

"What are you doing here? You don't have delivery service," I say.

"I do for my favorite customers." She smiles as she places the food and drinks on my desk. "Besides, Mitchell called me this morning and put in an order."

"Did he ask you to bring it over, too?"

She must hear the anger in my voice because she waves her hands in the air. "No, no, no. He definitely did not. In fact, he said he'd be by to pick it up around eight, but I wanted to see you, so I decided to deliver it myself instead."

"Well, thank you." I reach for my purse to get my wallet, but she stops me.

"Your boyfriend already paid, including a rather large tip." She shakes her head. "You really have to give him a lesson on how to properly tip someone."

"Oh, he knows. He also knows how hard you work and that you're one of my only friends, so I don't see the large tips ending anytime soon."

She sits down in the seat across from me. "How are you doing? Mitchell mentioned a certain officer has his sights set on you, and not in the good way like Mitchell does."

Mitchell divulged details of a case? That's so unlike him. But then again, this is Marcia. She'd do anything for me, so I can see why he'd tell her about Officer Andrews harassing me.

"I'll be fine. Everything he has is circumstantial."

"Well, if you need someone to accidentally spill some laxative into his morning coffee, you let me know. That would certainly keep him too busy to try to accuse you of anything." She laughs, and so do I.

"Thanks, but I think I'll be okay."

She stands up. "All right then. I've got to head back. I hate leaving anyone else in charge. I swear things always go wrong when I step out for even a minute."

"Thank you again for the delivery," I say.

"Anytime. Good luck with the case."

Mitchell walks in just as Marcia is walking out.

"Good morning, Detective."

"I was told you were here. I didn't intend for you to deliver the order," he says, holding the door for her.

"I know, but I wanted to say hello to Piper." She leans toward him, so I can't hear what she whispers, but I'm sure it's something about him looking out for me.

Mitchell comes over and sits down, grabbing his coffee from the caddy. "How did you sleep?"

"Not well. I've been thinking about it, and the entire mirror thing doesn't add up."

"You're right. I can't figure it out either. We know Austin doesn't work for the garbage company, so he didn't go through your trash."

It was the killer. It had to be. But why give the mirror to

Austin. Unless... "Austin had the same mirror from the same grooming set I own. The killer swapped my mirror for Austin's to plant my fingerprints at the murder scene. Someone is trying to get rid of me. Put me behind bars so I can't stop him."

"Fact?" Mitchell asks.

I shrug since I'm only guessing. "What other cases are open?"

"You think this guy has killed before? Like a serial killer and he's trying to keep us from connecting him to this crime by implicating you?"

Something about that feels wrong to me. "Maybe he didn't kill anyone else. Maybe it's not as big as that." I rub my forehead. "I don't know, but we need to figure this out fast. Officer Andrews is going to do everything in his power to have me arrested."

Mitchell places his hand on top of mine. "I'm not letting that happen."

I gently pull my hand away so I don't accidentally read him again. "It won't be up to you. You aren't the lead detective on this case."

"Then the chief will put an end to this lunacy."

"The chief? You mean the guy who put Officer Andrews on this case to begin with? The one who warned me any more evidence against me would render him unable to stop Andrews from arresting me?" Mitchell might not want to admit it, but the chief isn't going to come to my rescue. If and when Officer Andrews goes to him with more evidence, I'll be arrested. It's as simple as that.

"Then let's go talk to the garbage disposal company and get to the bottom of this." He stands up. "Where's your dad this morning?"

"I'm not sure, but if I had to guess, I'd say he's at the station."

"You think he's talking to the chief?"

"You got it." I stand up and place Dad's coffee on his desk with a note telling him where we've gone.

Mitchell grabs the pastry bag, and we're eating breakfast on the road in a matter of minutes.

"Garbage pickup is on Thursdays, so that's when the mirror was picked up in the trash," I say.

"Right. I have the two guys—the one who drives the truck and his partner—meeting us this morning. They got someone to cover their morning shift today."

"Oh, that's right. It's Thursday." The days of the week always jumble together when I'm working on a big case like this.

"Yeah. Did you forget to empty your garbage this morning?"

"Naturally. But that's the perk of living in an apartment complex. I just bring my garbage down to the dumpster whenever it gets full." As soon as I say it, I see the problem. "Anyone with access to that dumpster could have gone through my garbage."

"That's true, so there's no way to be sure the mirror was even in the garbage when it was picked up."

Which means this meeting isn't going to produce any leads. The garbage men aren't going to know anything. "Unless the person who took the mirror was lurking near the dumpster with my trash bag, these guys aren't going to be able to tell us anything."

"I know, but maybe you'll pick up on something."

The only way that will happen is if one of the men we're about to meet is the one who took my mirror, and that means I'm going to have to read them both to find out.

"Here we are," Mitchell says, pulling into the gravel lot where the waste disposal trucks are housed. There's a small building to the side of the lot, and I'm assuming that's the office.

We walk inside to a receptionist, who is currently on the phone. She holds up a finger when we approach. "Someone will be there just as soon as possible," she says into the phone. "We're a little short on drivers this morning. Yes, I assure you your garbage will be picked up today. Thank you." She hangs up and shakes her head before addressing us. "Sorry about that. Some of our customers get impatient when their garbage isn't picked up exactly on time, but we are short one crew this morning."

I look at Mitchell, knowing we're the cause of that. I guess they couldn't find someone to cover their shift during this meeting.

"I think we might be to blame for that," Mitchell says, pulling his badge, which hangs on a chain, from under his shirt. "I'm Detective Brennan, and this is my partner, Piper Ashwell. We have a meeting with two of your employees this morning."

"Oh, yes. Mr. Huhn told me you were coming. You can use the conference room down that hallway." She points. "First door on your right. I'll phone the two employees you'll be speaking with and have them meet you there." She picks up her phone.

"Thank you," Mitchell says before we walk down the hallway.

The conference room is tiny. It's just one table with five chairs around it. I'm guessing it was a large storage closet that was converted into a conference room. Mitchell and I sit down and wait. A few minutes later, two men in green uniforms enter the room. One is short with dark hair and a goatee. The other is medium height with red hair and lots of freckles.

"Are you the two detectives?" the redhead asks.

"Yes, I'm Detective Brennan, and this is Piper Ashwell," Mitchell says, extending his hand to each of them.

"I'm Mike, and this is Roger," the redhead says, making me think he's the driver. "I should mention Roger is deaf. He's great at reading lips, though, so make sure you're looking at him when you're speaking, and he'll be able to understand you just fine."

Mitchell pulls out his pad and pen. "Last Thursday, you emptied the dumpster at the apartment complex at this address." He turns the pad so they can see my address.

Mike nods. "Yup. That's on our normal Thursday route."

"Do you remember seeing anyone near the dumpster?" I ask, making sure to look at Roger.

Roger furrows his brow as if trying to remember. Then he shakes his head.

"Me neither," Mike says. "Why?"

"Something was stolen from that dumpster. We're trying to determine if it was taken before or after the dumpster was emptied."

"You mean like an ex or a stalker going through someone else's trash to see what they're up to?" Mike asks.

"Something like that," Mitchell says, clearly not wanting to mention this is in reference to a murder investigation.

"We actually see that a lot. It's true what they say. You can learn a lot about a person by going through their trash."

"Do you ever go through the garbage after you pick it up?" I ask.

"Me? Nah. We pick up the dumpster, leave an empty one, and drop off the full one. That's it. I don't want to go home to my wife and kids every night smelling like trash. You'd be amazed at what people throw out. You do not want to smell like it." Mike's face screws up in disgust.

"If you want my opinion, anyone stalking someone else's trash is going to grab it as soon as the person discards it. Long before garbage collection day." Mike's words make a lot of sense. So much so that my senses confirm that's what happened. Someone took my trash moments after I tossed it into the dumpster.

"Thank you both for your time," I say, standing up. "We won't keep you from your route any longer."

"Sure thing," Mike says.

Roger turns to Mike and starts signing.

"What's he saying?" Mitchell asks.

"Oh, he says to steal another person's garbage is a dirty, smelly job. Sometimes he wishes he had no sense of smell instead of no hearing."

No sense of smell. Something about that sends tingles throughout my body.

After saying goodbye, Mitchell and I head for his patrol car. I'm not sure if I should mention the weird feeling I got when Mike translated what Roger signed. It doesn't really seem to make much sense to me or have anything significant to do with this case.

"Dead end. What now?" Mitchell asks me.

"Maybe we track down Austin's bookie and see what he knows."

"Sounds like a good plan, but how do we find out who the bookie is?"

"Phone records, Detective. This one is on you. I'm sure Austin called the number numerous times."

"You know this means heading to the station," Mitchell says, getting into the car and starting the engine.

"Oh joy."

I'm a little surprised when we get to the station and Dad's BMW isn't there. I figured it might take him a while to convince Chief Johansen to not allow Officer Andrews to arrest me *and* have him removed from this case. So it either didn't go well, or the universe is smiling down on me and granted me this one favor. I'm going to put my money on the former.

"Hey, guys," Officer Wallace says as we enter the police station. I have to say, having him be the first officer you see when you walk in is very smart. He's the nicest officer at the station.

"Morning, Wallace. What's been going on around here?" Mitchell asks.

"Piper's dad was here talking to the chief. Someone else has been conveniently absent from the station."

"Did Andrews take the day off?" Mitchell asks.

Officer Wallace shrugs. "I'm not sure where he is."

"Probably out trying to convict me," I say.

Officer Wallace walks around his desk and stands awkwardly in front of me like he's trying to figure out if he should risk touching me. He finally settles on putting his hand on my shoulder. "Piper, your reputation is on your side. Andrews used to be a good cop, but ever since you came around, he's changed. You rattle him. We all see it. I don't think you have anything to be worried about. At the end of the day, what you can do far exceeds what he can do."

"Thank you, Officer Wallace. I appreciate that. But it looks like I'm up against more than just Officer Andrews. Someone seems to want to put me behind bars. Officer Andrews might be more than willing to do just that, but he didn't plant this evidence against me."

Officer Wallace leans toward me and whispers, "Are you sure about that?"

For him to question a fellow police officer says a lot. As much as I don't like Officer Andrews, I know he's not behind this. "I am sure," I say.

Officer Wallace nods. "You hear about crooked cops. I had to ask."

"What crooked cops are you asking about, Wallace?"

I don't have to turn around to know that Officer Andrews just overheard our conversation. Nor do I need my psychic abilities to tell me this will make him double his efforts to charge me with murder.

CHAPTER NINE

"Brennan, Ashwell, and Andrews, my office! Now!" Chief Johansen bellows.

I actually jump.

"Gladly," Officer Andrews says as he marches past Mitchell and me to the chief's office.

"I hope I didn't cause that," Officer Wallace says to me.

"You didn't. This has been a long time coming," I assure him.

Mitchell walks beside me, and I know he's trying to present a unified front against Officer Andrews, but we look ridiculous when we get to the chief's office and have to stop entirely since we don't fit side by side through the doorway. I give him a look, and he motions for me to go first.

"Sit. All of you. And close the door, Brennan."

Mitchell shuts the door but doesn't sit, a bold move considering he was directly ordered to. I take the seat farthest from Officer Andrews, leaving a space between us.

Officer Andrews starts to talk, but the chief shuts him down immediately. "No. It's my turn to speak. I don't want to hear a word from any of you." He pauses, I'm sure as a test to see if any of us is stupid enough to say something. No one does. "Good. Now we've done this song and dance before, and to be honest, I hate having to repeat myself. Andrews, you were supposed to learn something during your suspension. Instead, you come back here accusing one of our consultants of murder based on circumstantial evidence. In doing so, you make this department look incompetent. And Ashwell, instead of using your abilities to clear your name, you're running scared from a cop who is in serious danger of losing his badge."

Officer Andrews's mouth drops open. I don't think any of us were expecting the chief to go so far as to threaten anyone's job.

"And Brennan, I don't need to tell you how stupid you are for getting involved with your old partner's daughter, who happens to be a consultant for this police department. You are all giving us a bad name right now, and I have half a mind to dismiss all three of you from the case."

I reach out with my senses, trying to get a feel for what's about to happen. But damn it if I don't have good control over seeing the future yet. I do, however, pick up on Chief Johansen's anger mixed with a small amount of... desire for punishment.

"It's clear the three of you are incapable of coexisting in the same town, let alone working together on cases. So, here's what's going to happen."

I think we can all sense how bad this is going to be.

"You'll all continue to work on this case, and when it's over, one of you"—he motions between Officer Andrews and Mitchell—"will be transferred to the Tillboro Hills PD."

"What?" Officer Andrews blurts out. "Chief, please reconsider."

I look at Mitchell. Tillboro Hills isn't too far from Weltunkin, but it would still require him to move because of the hours he'd have to work. I just got used to having him around and calling him my boyfriend. If he moves away...

And would that mean I'd be stuck working with Officer Andrews when I assisted the WPD with cases? This is a nightmare on so many levels.

"I've considered this for long enough," Chief Johansen says. "I won't let any of you ruin the reputation of this police department. I suggest you solve this case quickly because one of you is going to need time to pack." He waves his hand in the air, indicating we're dismissed.

Mitchell and I leave the office and go straight for his desk. Officer Andrews walks right out of the station.

"He said one of us, so that has to be a hint that it's Andrews who's being transferred, right?" Mitchell asks me.

"I don't work here. He can't transfer me. He meant either you or Andrews, so his word choice wasn't giving away anything." I slump back in the chair. "We need to solve this case so you'll get to be the one who stays. Pull up the phone records."

"It will only take a second. Andrews already accessed them."

Great. That could mean he already identified the bookie, too. If he solves this case before us, Mitchell will be leaving Weltunkin.

I get up and look over his shoulder at the computer screen. Sometimes when I look at a list, certain names will pop out at me as being important. They look bigger and bolder than the rest. I'm hoping the same will apply for phone numbers right now. Mitchell scrolls through the list, and sure enough, one number stands out, and it was called multiple times.

"That's it," I say. "Write it down."

Mitchell scribbles the number on his notepad. "We don't have a name, and I doubt he's going to give it willingly when we call."

"Pretend you want to place a bet. Say you got the number from Austin Hawkins." It's actually the truth since the number came from Austin's phone records.

"Okay, that could work. In the meantime, I'll get

Wallace to trace the number and find out who it belongs to." He writes the number on a separate piece of paper and brings it to Wallace, who is all too eager to help us.

"I heard what the chief said."

I have no doubt the entire station heard. The chief's voice carries, even through closed doors.

"No one would be sad to see Andrews go, but you'd be a different story." he adds.

"Thanks, Wallace. I appreciate it," Mitchell says. Then he nudges my arm, directing me toward the door. "Call me when you have something for me."

"Will do." Wallace is already on his computer.

We get into the patrol car, and Mitchell takes out his cell phone. "Let's do this."

"Mitchell." I place my left hand on top of his, stopping him from dialing the bookie's number.

"Don't even think about apologizing to me, because you have nothing to apologize for."

"It's not that. I just... I don't want you to move away."

"I know." With the pad of his thumb, he wipes a tear that falls from my eye. He always seems to know how I feel before I do. Or maybe he's just saving me from the embarrassment of trying to put my feelings into words.

He dials the bookie's number and puts the call on speaker. It goes to voice mail, which doesn't surprise me because people doing illegal things don't answer calls from numbers they don't recognize. At the beep, Mitchell says, "Hey, I hope I have the right number. Austin

Hawkins told me to call you to place a few bets. If this is who he said it would be, call me back. I have a sizable amount I want to put down on an upcoming race." He hangs up.

"Smart not giving a name, but an upcoming race? Do you even know if there is a race coming up?"

"I'm assuming there must be some race coming up, whether it's horse racing, drag racing, or whatever other kinds of races people bet on. I was trying to be vague."

"Mission accomplished."

His phone rings, and since it's still in his hand, he turns the screen so I can see it. "It's him." He answers the call, placing it on speaker. "Hello?"

"Who is this?"

"You called me," Mitchell says. "Who am I talking to?"

"Hawkins didn't give you my name?"

"He said you wouldn't like that," Mitchell plays along.

"He was right."

"Okay, so what should I call you then?"

"How about Ebenezer?"

"Sounds good. You can call me Bob then."

The bookie laughs on the other end. "A man with a sense of humor and a love for Christmas classics. I like it. What can I do for you, Bob?"

"I recently came into some cash, and I thought betting might be a fun way to spend it. Maybe I'll even get lucky." Mitchell's doing a great job of disguising his own voice and playing the part of a guy looking to make some quick cash.

There's a part of me that's slightly worried he can pull off the lie so effortlessly, though.

"You mentioned a race. Do you mean this weekend's horse race?"

"That's the one. I'm going to play it safe and take the front runner."

"Safe bets don't make the best payouts," Ebenezer says.

"I'm just wetting my feet," Mitchell says. "Put me down for twenty grand."

Ebenezer whistles. "You come into an inheritance or something?"

"Or something. Hawkins said you're discreet. I hope that's true."

"Are you implying you won't be reporting any winnings to the IRS?" He laughs.

"You're a funny man, Ebenezer."

"I'll be in touch."

"Hang on a sec. I'm assuming you don't send checks, so where do I pay up if I lose?"

We need an address so I can meet this guy and read him to see if he was involved in Austin's murder.

"Like I said, I'll be in touch." The call ends.

Mitchell turns to me. "I don't suppose you were able to get any vibes from him through the phone."

I shake my head. "Sorry, Bob. I've got nothing."

Mitchell searches online for the next horse race. "The

race is tomorrow night, so I'll hear from Ebenezer after that."

"That's if you lose."

"Which at this point, I'm hoping for. But I'm guessing he'll call either way. Bookies usually want you to take your winnings and bet with them again. I'll hear from him."

"In the meantime, we can't sit idle. Officer Andrews is out there somewhere trying to catch a lead."

"All right, let's go back through what we know then. According to that email Austin sent you, he was scared someone was after him for the money he won."

The email! Why didn't I see this sooner? "Why didn't he say anything to me in the restaurant?" I ask. "If he really contacted me in fear that his bookie was trying to kill him, he would know what I look like, right?"

"Not necessarily. He clearly didn't go through your agency website. Otherwise, he wouldn't have emailed your personal account."

He's right. So how did Austin even find my email?

His email address is fake. "Oh my God."

"What is it?" Mitchell asks.

"Austin Hawkins never got in touch with me."

"What do you mean?"

"Whoever hacked into my personal email also created a fake account for Austin Hawkins."

"How do we prove that?"

"Austin probably had another email account."

"That doesn't prove he didn't have two. You have two email addresses."

"That's true, but we can find out when the second email account was opened."

Mitchell snaps his fingers. "I'm on it."

If it was opened close enough to the time of the murder, it would create some suspicion as to why a new account was used. It's still not real evidence, though. We aren't any closer to an answer than Officer Andrews is.

My phone rings in my purse, and a quick glance at the display shows Dad's picture. "Hey, Dad. Where have you been?" I ask, placing the call on speaker.

"I had a hunch after leaving the station this morning."

"What kind of hunch?"

"That Andrews was trying to pin this on you for a reason."

I scoff. "How about because he hates me? That feels like reason enough." I did get him suspended and threatened to tell his wife about his affair.

"Andrews is having money problems," Dad says. "He's made a few comments that led me to believe that to be the case, which is why I did some digging. Turns out he uses a bookie."

I cover my mouth with my hand. "He has the same bookie as Austin Hawkins."

"You got it, pumpkin. And worse, Andrews knew Hawkins."

"Knew him how?" Mitchell asks.

"My guess is if you follow Andrews once he's off the clock, he'll lead you straight to that bookie who's running an illegal gambling ring. That's where Andrews met Hawkins."

"Why do people do that when you can legally gamble in this state?" Mitchell asks.

"Dad, I'm not sure I want to know where you got all this information," I say.

He laughs. "Let's just say someone owed me a favor from a long time ago when I was on the force. I cashed in."

Something else comes to me as a truth. "The chief told you about the transfer, didn't he? That's why you called in this favor. You're trying to make sure Mitchell isn't the one who gets transferred to Tillboro Hills."

Dad clears his throat on the other end of the line. "Take me off speaker, Piper." Even though Mitchell hasn't said a word, Dad knew he was listening in.

I look at Mitchell, who nods. I take the phone off speaker and bring it to my ear. "Go ahead, Dad."

"Pumpkin, I've never seen you open up to someone the way you have with Mitchell. He makes you happy, and I'm not about to let anyone take that away from you. Now I'm not marrying you off just yet like your mother is, but I want you to be happy, and I know you wouldn't be if he left."

"Thanks, Dad." I can't bring myself to say anything else. Not with Mitchell sitting next to me.

"Go find Andrews and solve this case. Let him be Tillboro Hills's problem from now on."

"That's the plan."

"I'll go walk and feed Jez so you don't have to rush home for her."

"You're the best." I end the call. "Where do we start looking for Andrews?" I ask Mitchell.

"I'll call Wallace and see if he got a name connected to that number. I'll ask if Andrews is at the station, too." He makes the call. "Tell me you have something, Wallace." He pauses as he listens. "Well, that's certainly interesting. No wonder he screens his calls." He covers the mouthpiece and whispers, "The number belongs to a woman who has been deceased for four years."

"The guy's grandmother," I say, knowing it's true.

"Wallace, what's the woman's name again?" Mitchell gets out his notepad and scribbles the name. "Yeah, I got it now. Thanks. Hey, is Andrews at the station?" He looks at me and shakes his head. "Would you do me a favor and call me if he shows up? Thanks." He ends the call. "Wallace said Andrews hasn't been there all day."

"That could mean he's gone after the bookie already."

"Does that feel right to you?"

I lean my head back on the seat and clear my mind. "I'm ready for the game."

Mitchell waits a few seconds before starting to make sure I'm really ready. "What name did the bookie tell me to call him by?"

"Ebenezer."

"What model car does your dad drive?"

"BMW."

"What's your middle name?"

"Rose."

"Why is Andrews trying to pin this murder on you?"

"To protect his bookie."

"Is he afraid of this bookie?"

"Yes."

"Is Andrews in danger?"

"Yes."

"Is the bookie the killer?"

My eyes are open before he gets the last question out. "Andrews is in trouble."

"Do you think he'll be the next target?"

I nod.

CHAPTER TEN

Thursday night, no one hears from Officer Andrews, including his wife, who calls the station to ask about him. Friday morning, Mitchell, Dad, and I are in the chief's office.

"Now you're telling me the killer is going after Andrews next?" Chief Johansen asks me.

"She saw it while in a meditative state," Mitchell explains.

"You saw it?" he asks me.

"Well, not really. I just know it's true."

"How? If you didn't have a vision, then what was it?"

"It's how her abilities work. Kind of like an I spy, but... I don't know how to explain it. Like I spy with my psychic eye someone dead. Like that."

We all stare at him like he's suddenly grown another head, one that hopefully has a bigger brain than the one currently controlling his mouth. I can't believe he just spouted out another of his insane sayings in front of the chief! We must all look crazy now.

"Chief, I can't prove anything, but the fact that his wife reported him missing has to mean I'm right. He's in trouble. He..." Do I tell the chief about Andrews's illegal gambling? I don't like the guy, but tattling on him seems like a low thing to do when I know he's in danger.

"He what, Ashwell? If you know something, you need to start talking."

Dad laces his hands in front of him. "I uncovered a few things about Officer Andrews yesterday. I made Piper aware of these things, and she's trying to protect him by not mentioning the indiscretions now."

Chief Johansen laces his fingers together and places his joined hands on top of his shaved head. "You people are trying to drive me insane. First, you hate each other. Now you're trying to protect each other? I can't keep up."

"Actually, only Piper is trying to protect Andrews. He'd never return the favor," Mitchell says.

"And what about you, Brennan? Are you protecting Andrews, too?" The chief lowers his arms, resting them on the desk in front of him.

"Not at all. I'm doing my job."

"Good. Then why don't you fill me in?"

"Certainly, sir. Mr. Ashwell discovered Andrews is involved in illegal gambling and uses the same bookie Austin Hawkins was afraid of. Andrews was eager to pin the murder on Piper to keep suspicion off the bookie because, like Austin, Andrews is afraid of the bookie. I think that about covers it."

I hold up one finger. "Not quite. I'm pretty sure Andrews went to the bookie yesterday, and no one has seen him since."

"So the bookie is our killer, then," the chief says.

"Maybe. Maybe not," I say.

"What do you mean maybe not? All the clues point to that being the case."

"Sir, I think the person who hacked my personal email account also created a fake email address for Austin Hawkins. I think this person knew about Austin's gambling and wanted to create a trail that would implicate both me and the bookie to keep the police busy and cover up the real killer's tracks."

"You don't think the bookie killed Austin." It's not a question, but I answer him anyway.

"No, sir, I don't think the bookie is our killer. The killer has to be someone with access to the dumpster at my apartment building. He also has to have access to both Austin and Officer Andrews."

"The only connection between Austin and Andrews is the bookie!" Chief Johansen says.

"That's the only connection we know of right now, but that doesn't mean there isn't another."

The chief stands up and paces in the small space behind his desk. Then he steeples his fingers together and points them at us. "You three need to make finding Officer Andrews your top priority. If the killer is targeting him next, you need to find him before it's too late."

I don't mention that the killer might already have Officer Andrews because my senses aren't giving me a clear indication of whether or not that's true.

"I want regular updates. Now get out of here and find him."

"You got it," Mitchell says, looking way more confident than I'm feeling.

I eye him as we walk out of the office. "What are you up to?" I ask.

He smiles at me and approaches Officer Wallace's desk. "Wallace, we need Harry."

That's right! The WPD keeps an item belonging to each officer at the station in case of an emergency like this and Harry needs to pick up on their scent.

I smile and wink at Officer Wallace. "I've always said Harry is the best police officer at this station."

"That he is," Officer Wallace says, getting on the phone. "I'm getting his handler on the line now."

I turn to Dad and Mitchell. "Andrews left here yesterday in his patrol car. How will Harry pick up on his scent?"

"That's the tricky part. We'll need to hypothesize locations where he might have gone and bring Harry there to take over the search."

I don't point out that if we knew where Andrews

might be, we could go search there ourselves. Mitchell's only trying to help.

"Officer Wallace, can we call you with a location?" I ask.

"Sure. I'll get Harry prepped and ready in the meantime."

"Thank you." I turn for the door.

Dad and Mitchell hurry to catch up.

"Where are we going?" Mitchell asks.

"To Andrews's house to talk to his wife."

"Why? She doesn't know he's having an affair. I doubt she'll know what he does when he's not at work."

"That's a valid point, but if she can't answer our questions, some of Andrews's personal belongings will tell me all I need to know."

Mitchell smiles as we pile into his patrol car. Once again, I'm stuck in the back like a criminal. At least, Officer Andrews isn't around to enjoy the show. Dad has to let me out when we pull up to the house.

When we walk up to the front door, I reach out with my senses, trying to determine if there was any kind of struggle here. I don't pick up on anything, though, so I ring the doorbell. Mrs. Andrews recognizes us right away.

"Have you found Kurt?" she asks, and I can see she's been crying. Her eyes are puffy, and her cheeks are damp.

"No, Mrs. Andrews, not yet," I say.

"Please, call me Angela. Come inside."

Given that Officer Andrews doesn't believe in what I

do, I don't expect his wife to be open to me reading his belongings, so I try a different approach. "We were hoping we could see his study or home office. Maybe if we saw what he was working on, it will tell us where he might have gone."

She leads us to a small room near the kitchen. "I told him not to take on those types of cases. They put him in danger, but after that awful business with having to interview strippers, I think he wanted to avoid tainting his reputation by being put on assignments like those."

He lied to his wife about why he was frequenting the strip club. It's a wonder I've been able to keep his secret all this time. This poor woman deserves so much better, yet here she is crying over her husband's disappearance.

"Do you mind if we look around in here for a few minutes?" I ask her, hoping she'll take the hint that we don't want an audience. I need to spark a vision, and I'd rather she wasn't here for it.

"Not at all. Do whatever you need to do to find my Kurt." She holds out her arm, showing off the tennis bracelet on her wrist. "He just bought this for me. For no reason. It was just a gift because he loves me."

More like a gift because he feels guilty for cheating on her. But then I realize that he's been having money problems. How did he afford the bracelet? Unless, he just won a bunch of money like Austin did. I look at Mitchell, who appears to have reached the same conclusion, judging by the expression on his face.

I realize Dad is talking to Angela, and they've moved out of the room. I can always count on him to get me privacy when I need to have a vision. I open the day planner on the desk. It looks like it's in code or something. Nothing is written out. It's just random letters and numbers, yet I know they aren't random at all. They stand for something.

"Do you think the letters represent what he's betting on and the numbers are the amounts he's betting?" I ask Mitchell.

He looks over my shoulder at the planner. "That could be it." He steps to my side and stares at me. "Is there a reason you're avoiding reading something in here? And I mean reading as in the energy, not what's written."

"It's Andrews. Who knows what I'll see?"

"Piper, I can't blame you for not wanting to see him with...those women, but if you focus on this"—he taps the day planner—"you should only see what's related to his gambling."

"I know." I'm being a baby. I tilt my head from side to side, cracking my neck. Then I take a deep breath, release it, and place my right hand on top of the day planner.

Officer Andrews looks over his shoulder at the closed door before turning back to the planner on the desk. "I'm trying to keep you out of it. I know the deal. I'm not stupid enough to risk a good thing here. There's no need for you to be concerned. I won't let her find you. Besides, you didn't kill anybody, so you have nothing to worry about."

"Why do I feel like you're asking that last part more than stating it as a fact?"

"No question at all. Except whether or not you'll place that bet for me."

"Consider it done. Just don't let me down."

I open my eyes. "He was definitely protecting the bookie because he needs the money. I don't think he really believed the bookie killed Austin, but there was some uncertainty in his voice, like he wasn't a hundred percent sure."

"No ID on the bookie?" Mitchell asks.

"He didn't call him by name. I recognized the voice as the same person you spoke to, though, so the number my dad got is definitely correct."

Mitchell huffs out a breath. "Can you focus on a different date? Try yesterday since that's the date he went missing."

"Mitchell, I wasn't focused on any one date. I just allowed the energy on the day planner to show me what I needed to see." I wish I could read a person's calendar and find out everything they did that day. Boy would that make being a P.I. the easiest job in the world.

"How's it going in here?" Dad asks, poking his head into the room.

"Just confirmed what we already knew. The bookie is the connection, but there has to be more." I look around, but there's not much to read in this room. I step out and find Angela in the living room drinking iced tea.

"I thought you all might be thirsty. I could cut up some lemon if anyone would like." She starts to get up, but I shake my head.

"That's not necessary. We should get out there and find your husband. Another officer will be here shortly with his K9 partner to try to pick up on your husband's scent, but before we go I was wondering if you could tell me if Kurt had any routines. You know, ways to clear his head when he worked a difficult case." I need something other than going to a strip club because I am not willing to read the women or anything else in that place.

"He belonged to a gym."

"He did?" Mitchell and I both say. Andrews doesn't strike me as the gym membership type.

"It was a recent thing. He said it was good for stress relief. He even made a few friends there."

My senses go crazy, like a million ringing bells telling me to pay attention. "Which gym?" I ask.

"I forget the name, but it's the one at the corner of Fifth Street."

The one on the same road as my office and Marcia's Nook. "Thank you, Angela. We'll keep in touch if we find anything."

"Please do. I'm so worried about him." She sniffles again.

"We'll show ourselves out. Please don't get up," Dad says, patting her shoulder.

She nods and dabs her eyes with a tissue.

Once we're outside, I say, "It's the gym. That's the other connection. I think Austin is one of the friends Angela was talking about."

"So they work out together?" Mitchell asks.

"Maybe. They both go to that gym, though. Or they did."

"That might be how Andrews found out about the bookie," Dad says. "It's possible Austin mentioned it during a workout one day."

"True. Guys talk while lifting weights and such," Mitchell says, and Dad and I both turn to him.

"You belong to a gym?" I ask.

He flexes. "Is that so hard to believe?"

"Actually, yes. I see you practically twenty hours a day. When do you have time to go to the gym?"

"Okay, fine. I just joined last weekend."

When he was avoiding me because he thought I wanted space. "Tell me it's the gym on Fifth Street."

"It is. Why?"

"Because now we can go there as your guests and pretend we're checking out the gym because we're considering getting memberships ourselves," I say.

I spend the drive wondering why Officer Andrews would chance running into me by joining a gym so close to my office. Unless he liked the idea of keeping tabs on me. From past experience though, he prefers to keep his distance, so something isn't adding up. Of course, with my people skills, I didn't even notice him or the fact that there is a gym on the same street as my office. I like living in my little bubble. Life is much nicer there.

Mitchell brings us inside and checks in with the front desk, marking us down as visitors for the day. Becky, a peppy brunette wearing extra tight workout clothes, smiles at us and tells us to check in with her before leaving so she can answer any questions we might have. Dad and I just nod as we follow Mitchell into the weightlifting area.

"The other room to the right houses the treadmills, stair climbers, rowing machines, and other aerobic exercises. This one is strictly for free weights and lifting machines," Mitchell tells us. "The locker rooms are down that hallway there. Men are to the left, and women are to the right. Finally, there's a daycare area for parents to drop off their kids while they workout. That's just past the locker rooms at the end of the hallway."

I find it amusing that they keep the kids as far away from the people working out as possible. I guess it's smart, though. I look around the room, noting the racks of free weights and several machines I don't know the names of. When my gaze lands on the bench in the middle of the room, I'm immediately drawn to it.

"What's that called?" I ask, walking over to it.

"The bench press," Mitchell says. "Why?"

"My senses are drawing me to it."

Being that it's a weekday and most people are at work, the place is pretty empty. There's one guy in the corner using free weights and checking himself out in the mirrors, which line the walls. At least I won't have a large audience when I try to spark some visions. The biggest problem is going to be that countless people use this equipment, which means getting a read of any one person off of it will be nearly impossible.

"Can you sense either Andrews or Hawkins from it?" Dad asks me.

"No. Most of what I'm sensing is..." I'm not sure how to describe it. Testosterone? "I guess it's the force people put out when lifting the weight bar. It's not rage. It's pressure, resistance, and determination."

"Here," Mitchell says, moving to position himself behind the weight bar. "Lie down as if you're going to try to lift the bar."

"Lie down on the bench where countless sweaty people have been? Call me crazy, but I'm not exactly eager to do that." I wrinkle my nose in disgust.

"This is why we're here, isn't it?" Mitchell asks me.

I huff. "Fine." I sit down on the bench and immediately feel the man in the corner looking my way. I'm not in workout attire by any means, so I'm sure I look ridiculous to begin with. Couple that with the fact that it's obvious I've never lifted a weight in my life and the hundred and some pound weights on the bar, and I can see why I'm drawing the man's attention.

He puts his weights back on the rack, slings his sweat towel over his shoulder, and walks over to us. "You know what you're doing there?" he asks me. "That bar is likely holding more than you weigh." He gives Dad and Mitchell and admonishing look. "Are you too trying to get her hurt?"

"I'm her father," Dad says. "I'd never put her in a situation where she could get hurt."

"Besides, she's not going to lift the weights. She's just trying to envision herself working out here," Mitchell says, and I almost chuckle at his word choice. It's a good cover for what I'm really about to do, which is have a vision of hopefully Officer Andrews or Austin Hawkins.

The man holds up his hands. "Just making sure the lady isn't in any danger. I didn't mean to offend anyone."

"I appreciate the concern," I say.

The man smiles at me and walks out, leaving us alone.

"Let's get this over with," I say, lying back and reaching up to grip the bar above my head.

Mitchell is looking down at me. "Don't try to lift this. No matter what you see in the vision, keep your grip loose so nothing bad happens."

"Got it."

He grips the bar himself to be on the safe side.

I close my eyes. Several voices fill my ears all at once.

"Come on. One more."

"Woo! That was a hell of a bet."

"Don't give up on me. You've got this."

I open my eyes and let go of the bar.

"Did you see either of them?" Mitchell asks as I sit up.

"I didn't see anything. I heard bits of conversations.

There's too much energy on this bar from everyone using it. I can't place who was speaking, but one thing did stand out."

"What's that, pumpkin?" Dad asks.

"Someone commented on a bet that was made, and it sounded like they were impressed."

"So that could mean that either Hawkins or Andrews told someone here about the bets," Mitchell said.

"Or they were talking to each other," Dad says.

"Could you recognize the voice?" Mitchell asks.

"No. Everyone was talking all at once." I look at the weight bar behind me. Trying to read it again would most likely produce similar results. The only way I'm going to identify the person I heard talking about bets is to view a list of gym members. But getting that list is going to take the efforts of the biggest flirt I know. I stand up and face Mitchell. "I'm going to need you to flirt with perky Becky to get me the names of everyone who works out here."

"You're asking me to flirt with her?" He looks like a mouse caught in a trap.

"Believe me, I hate this idea as much as you do." I couldn't stand his flirting before we got together. I'm not sure how I'm going to endure it now.

CHAPTER ELEVEN

"Maybe we should wait here," Dad suggests to me. "Mitchell can go talk to Becky and let us know when he's finished."

I know he's trying to spare me from witnessing Mitchell's flirting, but I think it's worse to not know what he's saying and doing. "I'll be fine. It's just an act." I shrug like it's no big deal, but Dad can always see right through me.

He puts and arm around my shoulders. "I'm aware you know that *here*." He taps my head. "It's here that I'm worried about." He motions to my heart.

"I'm good, Dad. Really." Mitchell's slipped up and said the L-word to me, but I haven't said it back. I'm not ready to talk about that. I do trust Mitchell, though. "He's only doing this because I asked him to."

x

"Exactly. I'm not looking forward to this at all," Mitchell says.

"Then I guess we should get it over with." Dad starts for the front desk.

Mitchell reaches for me, but I pull away. "Becky will never fall for your flirting if she figures out we're together."

"Right." Despite his agreement, he still looks disappointed.

Becky smiles when we approach her. "So, what did you both think? Do you have any questions I can answer for you? Or are you ready to join and let us get you into the best shape of your lives?"

Mitchell leans on the desk and smiles. "Actually, they're still mulling it over. The decision was easy for me when I walked in and saw your beautiful face, but they might need more convincing."

Becky blushes and giggles. "Oh, stop." She flirtatiously swats at Mitchell's arm. "Oh my. I see someone has been getting in some time with the weight bars." She runs her hand along his bicep.

Dad pulls me toward the exit under the guise of showing me the workout clothing for sale. "Let's just face this way and allow Mitchell to get the info we need."

I thought I was finished having to watch women fawn all over Mitchell. Ever since we started dating, he's totally ignored any looks or flirtatious comments from other women. But he seems to have fallen right back into his old ways with Becky. It's a little too much to stomach.

Becky giggles again, and Dad puts his arm around me. "Relax your fists. You're supposed to look happy, not like you want to punch her in the face."

"But I *do* want to punch her in the face."

Dad chuckles and releases me. "Green is not your color, pumpkin. Remember he only has eyes for you."

"Just tell me when it's over."

"It's over," Mitchell says, coming up beside me.

I look up at him. "Did you get the list?"

"Please. Did you ever doubt me?" He smiles, wraps an arm over my shoulder, and leads me to the door.

"What are you doing?" I ask. "Isn't Becky supposed to think you're interested in her?"

"Not anymore. I got what we need. And in case you haven't noticed, I've never been good at hiding my feelings for you."

I look back over my shoulder at Becky, who is eyeing us with a furrowed brow. She probably thinks Mitchell is the type to hit on everyone, and that's mildly amusing considering that's what I originally thought of him, too. "I feel a little bad that we tricked her. Should I go apply for a gym membership or something?"

"Why? Do you not trust me to come here without you? Do you think I'll flirt with Becky?"

"No. Nothing like that." I do think Becky will try to flirt with him, though.

"Then let's go." Mitchell opens the door for me.

Once we're in the car, Dad asks, "What did you say to get the list of names from Becky?"

"I told her Piper wanted to ask around and find out which of her friends belonged to the gym before she committed to a membership. I said I wished I could get a list of the members because it would be so much easier to convince her if she could see a bunch of familiar names on the list."

"And naturally, Becky offered to help you out there," I say.

"She made me promise not to tell her boss or anyone else. It's 'our little secret.'" He makes air quotes.

"Isn't that just so special?" I roll my eyes, which makes Mitchell laugh.

"You really are jealous."

"She totally is," Dad says.

"Okay, enough out of you two. We have a case to work, or am I the only professional sitting in this car?" I cross my arms and lean back in the seat, realizing I probably don't look all that professional in the back of a patrol car. Maybe Becky is watching through the window and thinks I'm a criminal.

Mitchell pulls a paper printout from his pocket. "Here you go." He unfolds it and holds it up to the metal grate dividing the seats so I can read it.

I scan the list of names. Kurt Andrews and Austin Hawkins are both on it with their names in big bold letters —or at least they look that way to me thanks to my senses tuning in to them. Then another name pops out. "Cole Bailey."

"You think that's who you heard in your vision?" Mitchell asks.

"I don't know, but he's the only other name besides Andrews and Hawkins that's popping out as being important to the case."

"Then let's go look up Cole Bailey," Dad says.

Mitchell drives us back to the office. He goes next door to get us some coffee and food from Marcia's Nook while Dad and I start our search.

"Okay," Dad says. "I found a Cole Bailey living here in Weltunkin. His Facebook page mentions weightlifting as a hobby, so this could be our guy."

I slide my chair over to read his computer screen. Cole's profile picture is a cartoon drawing of the Incredible Hulk, so I have no idea what he looks like. "Any photos?"

"Not a one. His only posts are about how much he benched at the gym. It's like his own personal log of his workouts."

I slide back over to my desk and continue searching. There has to be something about him online.

Mitchell walks in balancing a drink caddy and white pastry bag in one hand while texting with the other. "I've got Wallace running the name through the system. If he doesn't have a record, it won't help, but we might find an address so we can go talk to the guy."

"We can't find any images of him online. Isn't that strange? I mean, I don't use social media, but when you search me, several photos come up." How has this guy managed to stay off the grid when we live in such a digital age?

"Piper, you've been in the newspaper for your work with the WPD, and your photo is on your website," Mitchell says, taking a seat across from me. "I know you like to forget that, but people know who you are."

Something about his words makes me pause. "Say that again."

"What?" Mitchell furrows his brow at me.

"Repeat what you just said." I close my eyes and take a few deep breaths.

"Which part? About your photo being in the paper and online?"

"No. What you said after that." I gesture for him to hurry up, and I continue to try to clear my mind.

"People know who you are."

Ding, ding, ding! "That's it. Cole Bailey knows me." I open my eyes to see Dad and Mitchell staring at me in confusion.

"We're going to need more than that, pumpkin. Where are you going with this?"

"He could be the one who went through my garbage."

"But why?" Mitchell asks.

"I don't know." My senses aren't giving me anything else. Just that Cole somehow knows me.

"Do you think he read about you?" Dad asks, and I know he's trying to get my senses to answer for me. The problem is they aren't because I don't know Cole Bailey. I don't know what he looks like, how old he is, or why he seems to know me. Until about thirty minutes ago, I didn't even know he existed.

"Here." Mitchell opens the pastry bag and pulls out a giant piece of pecan pie.

"This is new," I say, immediately opening the clear container and grabbing a plastic fork.

"Yeah, Marcia just tried a new recipe." Mitchell passes a slice of pie to Dad before digging into his own.

After eating a few bites of what has to be the tastiest pecan pie I've ever eaten, I tap the end of my fork on the container. "Do you think Officer Andrews talked to Cole Bailey about me? Maybe he vents about work while he's lifting at the gym."

Mitchell nods with his mouthful. Once he swallows, he says, "That would make sense."

Dad sips his coffee before saying, "Maybe Cole is just a nice guy who talks to everyone at the gym."

"He spots them, too," I say, shocking not only Dad and Mitchell but myself. "I was in the wrong position at the gym when I tried to have a vision."

Mitchell nods, picking up on what I mean. "I was standing in the spot you should have been in to read Cole. The hand positions on the bar for the lifter and the spotter are different."

"Do we think Cole is responsible for what happened to Hawkins?" Dad asks me.

I bob one shoulder and fork another piece of pie. "I don't know. It was too difficult to put any kind of emotion behind the phrases that were zipping through my head during the vision."

"Whispers," Dad says, referring to what I used to call my visions as a child.

"Yeah, that's exactly what it was like. Only the voices were loud, most likely because there's music playing in the gym and people have to talk over it."

"And a spotter would be talking loudly to encourage his partner," Mitchell says.

"Except they were talking about bets," I point out. "I don't think they'd talk too loudly about illegal betting."

"I still don't see why Hawkins and Andrews got wrapped up in illegal betting when they could have placed the same bets legally. Why take that added risk? Especially a police officer."

Mitchell's right. It doesn't add up. Unless... "Do you think Officer Andrews found out about the illegal gambling ring and tried to infiltrate it to make a bust?"

"And he decided to make a few bets in the process?" Dad asks.

I nod. "And when he actually made money, which we know he did since he bought his wife that bracelet, he might have ditched the idea of turning in the bookie and decided to protect him instead."

"Fact?" Mitchell asks.

I shake my head. "Sorry, no. I'm hypothesizing."

"It makes sense, though," Dad says. "We know Andrews isn't always on the up-and-up given how he steps out on his marriage. He could have been swayed to participate in illegal activity, too. Being a cop is a good cover."

"And the bookie might like the idea of having a cop looking out for him," Mitchell says.

"Wait. What if Officer Andrews is in trouble because the bookie didn't know he was a cop? What if he found out, and that's why Andrews disappeared?" I ask.

"Are you saying he ran from the bookie, or the bookie did something to Andrews?" Mitchell asks.

"I don't know. Again, I'm hypothesizing." We need more to go on than hunches. And there's only one place I'm going to get answers without having an address for Cole Bailey. "We need to go back to the gym so I can read that weight bar again, but this time I'll be in the position of the spotter."

After we finish our so-called lunch, we head back to the gym. Becky is still in flirt mode, and it's obvious she feels the need to compete with me for Mitchell's attention.

"It's so nice to see you twice in one day, Mitchell." She winks at him as if she believes she's the reason for his return.

"Well, Piper wanted to come back after seeing the list of names you gave me. I've just about convinced her to join, but she forgot to test out a few machines earlier and wanted to try them out now."

"Oh, well feel free to go on back, Piper. I can keep Mitchell company in the meantime." She leans forward on the desk, practically making her boobs pop out of her workout tank top.

"I wouldn't dream of letting her go in there without me," Mitchell says, reaching for my hand and lacing his fingers through it. "She'd have men hitting on her left and right. I can't let anyone think she's available, now can I?"

Becky stands up straight, her nostrils flaring now that she knows she was played. "I'll be needing that list back." She holds out her hand.

Mitchell removes it from his pocket and hands it to her. "Of course. Here you go. Thank you again for your help."

"And just so you know, the price of a membership just went up," Becky says, her tone lacking any friendliness as her eyes bore into mine.

"That's not a problem," Mitchell says. "If Piper decides to join, I'll happily pay the fee for her." He smiles at me, and we walk off toward the weight room.

"You two are always so entertaining," Dad says as we enter. "Poor Becky looked heartbroken back there, though."

"Forget heartbroken. She looked like she wanted to throw me through the wall," I say.

"I wouldn't have let her lay a finger on you," Mitchell

says. He must sense my tension because he immediately adds, "Not that I think you need my protection. I'm sure you could have handled her yourself."

Dad clamps a hand down on Mitchell's shoulder. "You're learning."

There are more people working out now, and the bench press is currently occupied, which means we have to wait our turn. Mitchell walks over to the free weights and picks up a conversation with a guy there. I'm not sure if he knows him or if he's trying to see if the guy knows Cole Bailey.

Dad strikes up a conversation with the guy at the bench press, standing in as his spotter. And that leaves me leaning against the mirrored wall, feeling and looking completely uncomfortable and out of my element.

To my surprise, Becky shows up with a clipboard in hand. She marches right over to me. "Visiting hours are over for the day, so if you want to stick around, you're going to have to sign up for a membership."

Visiting hours? She makes it sound like this is a hospital. "I didn't realize there were time constraints on the visitations. Can you show me where that's stated? I'm sure Mitchell would like to know for future reference, and I'd like to know as well in case I do get a membership and bring someone with me to check out the place."

Her jaw drops. She clearly didn't anticipate me questioning her on this made-up policy. "I'm sure it's on our website under terms and conditions. You can go on it yourself if you'd like to read it."

To her shock, I whip out my phone. "I'll do that. I'm waiting for the bench press to open up anyway." I pull up the gym's website and scroll through the terms and conditions. "Hmm. Maybe I'm reading this incorrectly or I'm not in the right spot because it doesn't mention time constraints on visitations. It just says it's one-day-only access."

"That means you can't come back tomorrow without getting a membership yourself," she says through clenched teeth.

"But I didn't come back on a different day. I came back on the same day, which complies with the terms on the website. I guess you were wrong." I put my phone away and smile at her.

She huffs, turns on one heel—because apparently heels are meant to be worn with workout attire—and stomps off.

"What was that about?" Mitchell asks me.

"That was me handling myself." I smirk.

"The guy I was talking to didn't know Hawkins. He doesn't know Andrews or Cole Bailey either."

A clang of the bar draws our attention to Dad, who is shaking hands with the guy who just finished his set. The man leaves, and Dad says, "He knows Cole. Works out with him on occasion. He said Cole is always here, and he spots a lot of people."

"He's always here, yet he wasn't around either time we came by? That seems fishy to me," I say.

"It could be proof that he's our killer," Mitchell says.

"Or it could be proof that his life is in danger, too."

"Are you saying Austin Hawkins death was just the first of many?" Dad asks me.

"That's exactly what I'm sensing."

CHAPTER TWELVE

Since there might be two lives at stake, I waste no time in moving into the spotter position behind the weight bar. I need to have a vision and try to find Cole Bailey. The problem is there's no way to cover up what I'm doing because I can't have Dad or Mitchell do a set while I'm reading the bar. The motion would most likely mess with my vision. I just have to hope everyone is too focused on their own workouts to pay attention to me.

I take three deep breaths and close my eyes.

"That's incredible. You hit the jackpot."

"Good thing, too. I would have been dead if I couldn't pay back what I owed." Austin Hawkins *grimaces as he pushes the bar back up.*

"What are you going to do with all that money?" Cole *asks, keeping his hands on the bar but not offering any help in lifting it.*

"Not sure yet. I can't exactly put it in the bank, though. That might raise questions I don't want to answer."

The bar rises under my hands, and the vision ends. I open my eyes to see Mitchell lying down in the position Austin was in during my vision. Mitchell must have stepped in because people were staring at me.

"Get what you need?" he asks me, lowering the bar back into place and sitting up.

"I'm not sure." I sit down on the bench next to Mitchell. "I saw Cole spotting Austin. Austin told him about the bet that got him out of debt with the bookie. Cole seemed interested in what Austin would do with the money."

"Then that could mean Cole killed Austin to get his hands on the money," Mitchell says.

I shake my head. "I don't think so. Cole seemed like a good guy."

"That's what the man I talked to before said," Dad says, crossing his arms. "He said Cole helped out everyone. He's a friendly guy."

"Was he friendly or pumping people for information?" Mitchell asks. He has a tendency to see the worst in people sometimes, but since Cole could be a suspect, I get why he's questioning it.

"We need an address for him," I say. "And we know Becky isn't going to give you anyone's personal information." I bump Mitchell's shoulder with mine.

Mitchell's phone rings. "Brennan." His gaze meets

mine, and he mouths, "Johansen." "Yes, sir, I'm aware. I know how it looks, but we're working on it. In fact, we believe someone else might be missing as well. We're looking into Cole Bailey. He, Andrews, and Hawkins all belong to the same gym. We're here now. Yes, she's doing her thing. That's how we got this lead. No. I'm absolutely sure. Not a doubt in my mind. I'll keep you informed." He hangs up.

"Let me guess. He's not happy that one of his officers is missing or the fact that it could be used as a case against me since it's known Andrews hates me."

"He can't possibly think you'd do something to Andrews," Dad says, but the look on Mitchell's face says otherwise.

"He questioned if Piper threatened to tell Andrews wife some things and that's why he's disappeared."

"He thinks I gave Andrews an ultimatum. Leave for good or I'll wreck his marriage and reputation." I lace my fingers together.

Mitchell nods. "We need to find Cole Bailey if we can. We know this place is what connects everyone, and with Hawkins dead and Andrews completely MIA, Bailey's our best bet."

Except I'm pretty sure he's MIA in the same way Officer Andrews is.

———

We spend the rest of the day researching. I send Dad home for dinner, and Mitchell comes to my apartment so we can continue to work.

He gets a text just as we're finishing our pork lo mein. "It's Wallace. He said the emails both from Austin Hawkins and your personal email account were sent from a computer in the library," Mitchell says. "The same computer, which confirms they're fake."

"So we can't figure out who sent them." My name might be cleared, but we're no closer to finding the person who did this.

"Unfortunately, no."

Well, that's just great. I pull my legs up on the couch and pet Jez, who is curled up between Mitchell and me.

"Wallace also said Andrews's wife has been calling the station. There are no leads on where he might be. Chief Johansen has officers out searching for Andrews's patrol car. We can't seem to track it anywhere."

"Our only option is to go back to that gym and find out more about Cole Bailey." I get up and put our empty food containers in the garbage. Since I'm wearing lounge clothes instead of my work clothes, I'll actually pass for someone working out this time.

"Becky's not going to like this," Mitchell says with a small laugh, and he's not wrong.

The second we walk back into the gym, Becky looks up from her computer, and her head begins to shake back and forth so hard I'm afraid she'll give herself whiplash.

"Oh no." She walks around the desk and steps in front of me to block my path. "You are not coming back here a third time without paying for a membership. You're abusing the system at this point."

"Becky," Mitchell says, going right into charm mode.

I hold up my hand to stop him. "No, she's right." I put as much fake sweetness into my voice as possible. "I'd like to apply for a membership, please."

She crosses her arms. "You can't be serious."

"Oh, unfortunately, I'm very serious. What's the shortest amount of time I can sign up for?"

"Six months, but we reserve the right to revoke membership at any time if you don't adhere to the A Whole New You rules."

I jerk my head back. "What on earth are A Whole New You rules? Is that some new-age exercise lingo?"

Becky looks to Mitchell. "Is she joking?"

"Afraid not," he tells her before turning to me. "Piper, the gym is called A Whole New You."

"Seriously?" I look around and realize what I thought was a stupid slogan on all the shirts and other gear is actually a company logo. "Oh, I see."

"You've been here three times today, and you didn't even know what the gym is called? Why are you here? You obviously don't want to join."

Mitchell gives me a look to let me know he's got this. "Becky, what if I promise you'll never have to see Piper in here again if you just allow her to come in with me now? Please? As a favor to me?" He bats his perfect eyelashes at her. I mean really. Why are some men gifted with long, luscious eyelashes? It's kind of unfair. I might not be a makeup kind of girl, but I'll take those lashes any day.

"Fine," Becky says, "but I swear this is the last time. You could lose your membership over this too, you know." She wags a finger in Mitchell's face.

"Cross my heart," he says, adding the gesture, which seems to melt Becky on the spot.

I roll my eyes as she steps aside. When Mitchell widens his eyes at me, I say, "Thank you," to Becky.

We go directly to the weight room. Since it's evening and most people are done with work for the day, there are several people around. We start with the two at the bench press since that's where I'll most likely get the best read on Cole Bailey. The couple lifting are a woman with a blonde pixie cut and a guy wearing a tight white tank top, showing off the tattoos running across his shoulders and down both arms.

We stand against the wall of mirrors next to the bench, close enough for the couple to overhear us. Then Mitchell makes a show of looking around the weight room. "I might need you to spot me today," he says. "I don't see Cole anywhere."

The guy on the bench sits up and wipes his face with a towel. "If you need a spot, we just finished. I could spot you."

"Oh hey, that would be great," Mitchell says. "As long as you don't mind."

"Nah, it's no problem." The guy stands up and moves to the spotter position.

Mitchell adjusts the weights before lying down on the bench. "I haven't had much luck running into Cole lately," he says, getting into position.

"Yeah, he's been dragging me here instead," I say since I figure it might seem odd if I don't contribute to the conversation at all.

"I haven't seen Cole lately," the woman says, coming to stand beside me.

I want to find out if Cole was into betting as well, so I say, "He was so excited he won that bet. Maybe he went somewhere to celebrate."

"Cole placed a bet?" the guy spotting Mitchell asks. "That doesn't sound like him. He's really careful with his money."

So Cole isn't a gambler like Hawkins was. "I guess he wouldn't take an impromptu vacation then," I say.

"No, not him," the woman says. "Besides, this place is kind of his life. I'm a little worried that no one's seen him."

"Doesn't anyone have his number?" Mitchell asks, finishing his set and sitting up. He rubs his chest, which I'm assuming is sore under the strain of the weights.

The woman shrugs. "Cole's like our resident therapist. He listens to all of us vent about our troubles and he gives good advice, but he doesn't talk much about his own life."

"Yeah, I noticed that as well," Mitchell says, playing along.

"Time for your next set," the guy says, motioning for Mitchell to lie back down on the bench.

"I hope he didn't leave town," the woman says.

"What makes you think he would?" I ask since Mitchell is obviously straining with the workout.

"Well, he just sort of moved here one day. No one knows from where. He's kind of a mystery, but he's a really nice guy. Everyone seems to like him."

"I always got the sense he was running from something," the guy adds as he helps Mitchell place the weight bar back. "Not like he was in trouble but like something happened in his past that he couldn't deal with."

His mother died. The answer comes to me immediately. "I remember him saying his mother died recently. Maybe he didn't want to stick around where it happened, you know," I say.

Mitchell looks at me as he stands, and I give a slight nod to let him know I'm sure of that.

The guy slings his sweat towel over his shoulder. "That makes sense. He's really routine, kind of like he's moving through life on autopilot. It could be how he copes."

"Routine how?" Mitchell asks.

"He always used the same locker, did the same lifting routine, that kind of stuff."

"He even wore the same outfit every time he was here," the woman adds. "Though that might be a sign of money issues.

Yes. My senses key in on that as well, and I know for certain that Cole goes through other people's trash in hopes of finding things he needs and can't afford to buy.

"Did he use the locker on the end?" Mitchell asks. "That one always sticks for me. I have trouble getting my stuff out."

The guy shakes his head. "He likes the one in the middle. Dead center on top."

"Hey, thanks for the spot." Mitchell shakes the guy's hand. "We should probably get going if we're going to catch that movie," he says to me as he stands up. "I just want to take a quick rinse in the shower first." He motions toward the locker room, and I know what he really wants to do—sneak me in there so I can read the locker Cole always used.

"Yeah, let's go. It was nice talking to you guys," I say, giving them a small wave.

We walk toward the locker room, and I whisper, "Cole doesn't have much money, so he dumpster dives. He went through the dumpster at my apartment complex and took the mirror."

"Probably because it was in perfect condition," Mitchell says.

"Yeah. He probably had it here at the gym, and since he's a good guy, when Austin mentioned he thought he was being followed, Cole gave the mirror to him so he could watch behind him."

"We have to get you into the men's locker room." Mitchell pauses at the door. "Stay here and let me scope out the place first."

I nod and wait as he goes inside. I wave to the couple we just spoke to as they walk by on their way out.

Mitchell pokes his head out. "Someone's in the shower, but no one is by the lockers. We have to hurry."

I duck inside, and Mitchell leads me to the row of lockers.

"This one is dead center," he says, pointing to it.

I waste no time placing my right hand on the locker.

Cole holds a rosary in his hand. "I'm trying to do what you said, Mom. I really am. It's just hard when all my money went to those doctors. And they couldn't even save you. I left Ohio, though, and took your maiden name. I'm going to start over and try to live the life you want me to."

The next thing I know, I'm ripped from the vision and Mitchell's lips are on mine. I open my eyes and am about to berate him, when someone whistles.

Mitchell turns to the man stepping out of the shower area with nothing but a towel wrapped around his waist. "Sorry, man. Didn't realize we weren't alone in here."

The guy laughs. "She must be a hell of a kisser if you didn't even hear the shower running." He laughs and goes to his locker.

Mitchell puts his hand on the small of my back and

leads me out of the locker room. "Sorry about that. I didn't know what else to do when he walked out of the showers."

My face must be a million different shades of red. "It's okay. I found out Cole is from Ohio, and he's going by his mother's maiden name now."

"That's why we can't find him anywhere. It's not his legal name."

"Exactly. I think he's on the run from a lot of medical bills for his mother. I'm getting the sense she didn't have insurance and he might have lied to some doctors to try to get her treatment."

"Which obviously didn't save her life."

"Nope." Poor Cole. I can't help feeling sorry for him. All he wanted was to save his mother's life, and now he's paying for it in more ways than one.

"Let's get out of here. It's getting late," Mitchell says.

He's right. It is getting late, and I just hope it's not too late to save anyone else from being killed.

CHAPTER THIRTEEN

"Hey, isn't that the race you bet on tonight?" I ask, walking into the living room where Mitchell is watching a horse race.

"Yeah, which means I should hear from Ebenezer."

"That might give us some answers." I lean my head back on the couch. My hair is damp from my shower, and normally it would annoy me to go to bed with wet hair, but I'm exhausted. Not being able to make sense of a case is beyond frustrating, and that takes a toll on my energy levels. I was hoping a shower would wake me up a bit so Mitchell and I could brainstorm more on this case. No such luck. "Will you text me if he gets in contact with you tonight?"

Mitchell laughs. "No. You're going to bed, and I'll fill you in in the morning."

"But—"

"Come on." He takes my hand and pulls me to my feet. "Off to bed with you. Jez can walk me out."

"You can text me. If I'm sleeping, I won't see it until the morning anyway."

He kisses my cheek. "And you *will* be sleeping, so what's the point? Go to bed. I'll see you first thing in the morning." He kisses me again but this time lightly on my lips.

"Goodnight," I say, knowing I won't win this argument. "You better be at the office with coffee and donuts before I get there. Don't keep me waiting."

"I wouldn't dream of it."

———

I grip the weight bar in my hands and let the vision wash over me. But this time it isn't Cole or Austin that I see. It's Mitchell. He's lying on a cement floor, staring up blankly, a single bullet hole in his forehead.

"No!" I bolt upright in bed.

Jezebel jumps up and bathes my face in kisses.

"Oh my God." My entire body is shaking, and I reach out with my senses, trying to figure out if what I just experienced was a nightmare or something more. I'm too rattled to sense anything, so I grab my phone off the nightstand and call Mitchell.

It rings four times and then goes to voice mail. I end the call, clutching the phone in my left hand.

"No. This isn't real. It can't be. It has to be a mistake. He's probably in the shower. Yeah. He's showering and then he'll grab breakfast at Marcia's Nook and meet me at the office, right, Jez?" I turn to face her, twisting my pinky ring to try to calm myself.

Jez just cocks her head at me.

I quickly get dressed and feed and walk Jez before going to the office. I don't see Mitchell's patrol car in the parking lot, which sends my nerves into hyperdrive. I try his phone again, but the same thing happens. Four rings and then sent to voice mail. This time, I leave a message. "Mitchell, where are you? I've been calling you, but I keep getting your voice mail. I'm at the office, where you're supposed to be by now. Call me as soon as you get this message." I end the call and dial Dad.

"Good morning, pumpkin. I'm almost to the office. Do you want me to pick up breakfast on the way?"

"Have you heard from Mitchell?" I ask.

"No. Why?"

"He's supposed to be here, and he's not answering his phone." I unlock the office door and hurry inside, flicking on the lights and tossing my purse on the desk.

"Maybe he overslept."

Not likely. "I have a bad feeling, Dad." Dad never questions my feelings.

"Okay, I'll be there in three minutes. Don't move, and try not to panic."

Too late to not panic. I put the phone down and start

pacing. What if he heard from the bookie and went to meet him? What if he was in an accident? What if what I saw in my dream was real?

Tears spill down my cheeks.

"Piper." Dad rushes into the office and wraps his arms around me. "Tell me what happened."

"I saw him dead, Dad. I don't know if it's a premonition or if I'm just terrified of losing him, but I woke up this morning after seeing him on the ground with a bullet hole in his forehead." As soon as the words leave my mouth, I break down in a fit of sobs.

Dad hugs me tightly. "We don't know if it was real or not. We need to think logically about this."

"If he met up with the bookie and something happened..."

He pulls away and looks me in the eye. "You said you didn't think the bookie was the killer. Has that changed?"

I shrug. "I don't know. I can't think straight."

He brings me to my desk chair and sits me down. "Of course not." He wheels his chair over to mine and takes my left hand in his. "Why don't you let me do the thinking, and if anything I say triggers a response from your senses, you let me know. Okay?"

I nod, but I'm not sure my senses will be of any help in the state I'm in.

"All right. Maybe the bookie asked him to meet up this morning and said not to bring his phone."

"Mitchell would have texted me to say he'd be late coming to the office."

Dad nods. "You're probably right." He rubs the scruff on his chin as he thinks. "Okay, what if he got up early and went to the gym to see if Cole Bailey was there?"

"Again, he would have told me. I asked him to text me last night when he heard from the bookie, but he refused to because he thought I needed to sleep." I reach up and grab the sides of my head. "Why doesn't he ever listen to me?"

"Piper, not everything you say comes from your abilities. You didn't tell him to text you because you sensed something would happen. You told him to text you because you lo—"

"Don't use that word, Dad."

"Why are you so afraid of it, pumpkin? You know he loves you."

My stomach churns. "Then isn't that more proof that something happened to him? He wouldn't make me worry like this. Not intentionally."

Dad sighs and lowers his head. "We need to go to the station and tell the chief."

Two missing police officers. Possibly two dead police officers. I turn and throw up into my garbage can.

I spend the drive to the station trying not to puke on Dad's leather seats, but I'm pretty sure my stomach is empty after the display in my office. The station is virtually empty when we arrive. Officer Wallace is gone, and I know without a doubt that Harry is with him searching for Officer Andrews. That's what they've been doing for days now. Searching everywhere they think he might have gone.

Dad and I walk directly to Chief Johansen's office, and Dad knocks on the open door.

Chief Johansen looks up from the paper he's reading. "Thomas, Piper, what brings you here?" His gaze zeroes in on me, and he stands up, hurries to shut the door, and says, "What happened?"

"Mitchell is missing," I say. "I don't know if it was a premonition or not, but I saw him...dead."

Chief Johansen grabs a box of tissues from his desk and hands them to me. He sits on the edge of the desk and crosses his arms. "Tell me everything."

I fill him in on the fake bet in an attempt to make contact with the bookie, and the chief goes ballistic.

"He shouldn't have gone alone. An undercover operation like this is not a one-man job. He should have had backup, and at the very least, I should have known about this!"

"We understand protocol wasn't followed," Dad says, "but right now we need to find Mitchell. You can punish him later."

"If he's still alive," I say with a shaky voice.

Chief Johansen looks directly into my eyes. "You can't tell if what you saw has happened yet?"

"I don't know if it was a vision at all. I was asleep, and

I was so upset I couldn't make sense of it. But he won't answer his phone, and he never showed up at my office this morning even though that's where we planned to meet."

The chief stands up, walks around the desk, and picks up his phone. "I need you guys on the lookout for Detective Brennan as well as Officer Andrews. Yes, that's what I said. I want to know the second you find either of them." He slams the phone down so hard the entire thing topples over onto the floor.

"I've got rookies out there doing work I need seasoned cops for!"

He needs Mitchell.

I need Mitchell.

The chief whirls around and places both palms flat on his desktop. "What now? Tell me you can find him, Piper."

"I need a personal item of Mitchell's. I'll read it and try to locate him that way."

"Then go!" He points to the door.

Dad and I hurry out. I don't have a key to Mitchell's place, and the only items he keeps at my apartment are things he doesn't use often, so I won't get a good enough read off them. I go over to his desk and search it for something that might work.

"Pumpkin, I know this is going to sound strange, but you and Mitchell are together. Do you think it's possible for you to sense him all on your own?"

Oh God, he could be right. If my nightmare really was

a vision, *I* could have been what triggered it. My connection to Mitchell. I look at my father through tear-filled eyes. "Daddy."

"I know, pumpkin." He wraps his arms around me again. "Tell me what you need. How can I help you find him?"

What I need is Mitchell to walk through that door with some lame excuse about how he forgot to charge his phone and the battery died. But that's not going to happen. And the ache I'm feeling in my chest is telling me I need to find Mitchell fast, or my nightmare is going to turn into a reality.

CHAPTER FOURTEEN

"I can't do this here," I say, standing up.

"Where do you want to go?"

I want to go to Mitchell's condo. I want to be surrounded by his things. "I'm going to use my lockpick kit to get into Mitchell's place."

Dad doesn't question me. He just drives me to the condo. I never thought I'd use the lockpick kit I always carry in my purse to break into Mitchell's condo, but desperate times and all that. God, I even miss Mitchell's corny sayings. I'd give anything for him to butcher a common expression and turn it into some cheesy reference to me psychically solving crimes.

"Do you need help?" Dad asks since I'm not having much luck picking the lock. "I am the one who taught you how to do that."

I hand the tools to him, and he has the door open in a

matter of seconds.

"What do you want to try reading?" Dad asks, but I'm already heading to the bedroom. He follows me. "Should I be concerned that you headed directly in here?"

"No. When you made Mitchell babysit me twenty-four seven, he slept on the couch and insisted I take his room. That's how I know this is here." I pick up the photograph of me sitting on Santa's lap. "Mitchell played Santa after the guy who was supposed to do it wound up dead."

"That was your Christmas getaway vacation," Dad says.

"Yeah." Not that I got away from anything considering I wound up solving a murder.

"But you couldn't get away from Mitchell." Dad smiles. "We're going to find him."

"Don't make promises you can't keep." I take a deep breath, my chest shuddering from the fear of what I might see. Then I close my eyes and transfer the photo to my right hand.

Mitchell is sitting on the ground with his hands cuffed behind him. Officer Andrews is beside him. Both are gagged.

My own tears pull me from the vision.

"Piper?" Dad asks, thinking I've seen the worst, but really these are tears of relief.

"Mitchell's alive. So is Officer Andrews. They're together."

"You're sure what you just saw is happening now?"

I nod. "It felt that way."

"Did you see where they are?"

I shake my head. "I was pulled from the vision too quickly. I just saw that they're cuffed and gagged on the ground."

"We need a location, pumpkin. Can you try again?"

I nod and look at the photo, concentrating on where Mitchell is in this moment.

His image comes into view. He's sitting on a concrete floor. There's wood paneling on the walls, like it hasn't been redecorated since the 1970s. Mitchell is rubbing his face against the wood paneling, trying to force the gag out of his mouth.

The vision ends.

"No! I still don't know where they are."

"Tell me what you did see," Dad says. "Maybe we can figure it out together."

"The floor they're sitting on is cement."

"Okay, so it could be a factory or a basement."

"And the walls have wood paneling."

Dad's head jerks back. "That's interesting. I can't think of anywhere in town that has wood paneling."

"I need to try again." I clutch the photograph in my right hand, but Dad takes it from me.

"Piper, no. That's enough for now. I know you want to find him, but if you wear yourself down, you'll be no help to him."

"But I haven't found out anything useful. I can't give up. We can't search places to see who has wood paneling. It would take us all weekend to go into every building in Weltunkin. I don't know how much time he has. I have no idea who took him or what they want with him."

Dad puts the photograph back on the dresser and takes me by both arms. "Pumpkin, I need you to calm down. I know you didn't get the feeling that the bookie killed Hawkins, but all signs are pointing to it being the bookie who took Mitchell and Andrews. Now, maybe you're right and someone else killed Hawkins. That would be a good sign. The bookie might just be trying to intimidate Mitchell and Andrews. He might not actually hurt them."

"Whoever has them cuffed them with their own handcuffs. That means this person knows they're cops."

"Okay, but we already knew the bookie was aware Andrews is a cop."

It was probably Andrews who ratted out Mitchell. "One more try, Dad. I can do this."

He rubs his forehead, and I realize I got that trait from him. "Last try. If we don't get anything, we start searching the old-fashioned way."

"Deal." I pick up the photograph again.

Mitchell has the gag partially out of his mouth. "This is all your fault, Andrews. It's only fitting you wound up here."

Someone walks into the room. A tall man in his mid-

thirties. "Hey, how did you get this out of your mouth." He fixes Mitchell's gag and then hits him on the side of the head with the butt of his gun.

I wake up in Mitchell's bed hours later. My head feels like it's been bashed in. Experiencing things inside visions isn't real, but the pain I feel from it certainly is. I can't seem to convince my head that it wasn't actually hit with the butt of a gun. Mitchell's was.

Mitchell. I bolt upright and have to grab my pounding head. The room is spinning. "Dad?" I call out.

He rushes into the room and sits down on the bed. His hand goes to my head since I'm holding it. "What happened?"

"Mitchell. He managed to get his gag off. He was talking to Andrews. He blamed him for them being caught and said it was fitting that Andrews would wind up there."

"Did he mention where that was?"

I go to shake my head but stop when I cringe in pain.

"I'm getting you some aspirin, and don't even think about protesting. You won't be having any visions in this condition anyway, so I don't want to hear that aspirin affects your abilities." He's already off the bed and heading for the bathroom.

I can't help wondering if what Mitchell said was a clue. What place in Weltunkin would be fitting for Andrews?

Dad returns with two aspirin and a glass of water.

"Here." He hands them to me, and for once, I take them without complaint.

"We need to play the game, but a little differently this time," I say.

"I'm not sure you're up for that, pumpkin. You've been out cold for hours. If you'd slept any longer, I was going to bring you to the hospital for a possible concussion."

"I'm not the one with the concussion, but Mitchell might be. We don't have time to wait."

He lets out a long breath before saying, "Fine. Tell me what you want to do."

"Mitchell might have given me a hint, so I have to figure out what it is. We need to think of places that would be fitting for Andrews to go to."

Dad scoffs. "I can think of one, and I'm sure you can, too."

"Of course. The strip club. Do you know if they have wood paneling on the walls?"

Dad holds up both hands. "I've never set foot inside the place."

"We need to go."

"We need backup. We'll take this information to Chief Johansen."

I groan because that's going to waste that time that Mitchell might not have. But I also need more time for this aspirin to kick in. "Let's go."

The station is still practically a ghost town. Every

available officer is searching for two of their own. The chief spots us immediately and motions us into his office.

"What do you have for me?"

We sit down, and I fill him in on my visions and our theory.

He leans back in his desk chair. "I see. I guess there's only one thing to do. You're going undercover."

"What?" I ask, totally confused since I was never on the force and Dad has been retired for a while now.

"You heard me, Piper. You're going to get yourself a job at that strip club if that's what it takes to get you in there."

"Chief, you have reason to suspect two of your officers are in there. That gives you probable cause to storm in there and search for them. Why aren't you doing that?" Dad asks, his face red, and I'm not sure if it's due to the idea of his daughter working in a strip club or anger that the chief would assign me to a dangerous undercover case.

"Thomas, you know as well as I do that this can quickly turn into a hostage situation if we announce our presence at that club and demand entry. I'm trying to keep my men safe. This is the best way to do that."

"He's right, Dad. I hate this just as much as you do. No, I hate it more because I don't want to go anywhere near that place, let alone try to work there. But we're talking about Mitchell."

Dad pats my knee, but he addresses Chief Johansen.

"If she's going in there, I want her to have backup. One of your officers needs to be with her."

"I can spare Officer Gilbert. He knows Piper, and since he's new, most people at the club won't recognize that he's a cop."

Officer Gilbert loves my father, so I have no doubt he'll jump at the chance to help out with this case. I look at Dad and nod to let him know I'm okay with this.

"If anything happens to my daughter, Chief, you will have to have me arrested for murder. That is if you aren't the one I kill."

Dad should not be threatening the chief of police, but to my surprise, Chief Johansen doesn't admonish him. He simply nods.

Forty minutes later, I'm dressed in an outfit Officer Gilbert picked up at a costume shop on his way back to the station. I think the costume was meant to be a disco girl or something, but it's so tight on me—since he bought a child's size—that I definitely look like a prostitute. Not that I'm calling strippers prostitutes. Still, I think the outfit will at least get me through the door.

I'm pretty sure I see some of Dad's hair fall out when I walk out of the bathroom in the station.

"Well..." Chief Johansen clears his throat. "I guess you're all set then." He turns his attention from me and calls, "Gilbert."

"Ready to go, sir." Officer Gilbert is dressed in street clothes so he looks like a patron and not a police officer.

His eyes widen when he sees me, but he refrains from commenting on how I look.

"I'll be in the parking lot," Dad tells Officer Gilbert. "If anything goes wrong, I better get a call or a text or something."

"Yes, sir, Detective Ashwell." Officer Gilbert salutes him.

"I want updates," Chief Johansen calls after us as we walk out of the station.

Officer Gilbert drives us in his car, which is a beat-up black sedan. "Sorry about the car. I was going to get a new one, but I haven't been on the force long, so money's a little tight. And I figure I drive a patrol car when I'm a work, so I don't really use this car much at all."

"It's fine," I say, hoping he'll stop rambling. He's a nice guy, but he's also extremely eager, especially when my father is involved in any way. It can be a bit much to take at times.

"So, you and Brennan. How's that going?" he asks.

"Well, he's currently being held hostage in a seedy strip club, so not great at the moment." When Officer Gilbert gives me a confused look, I say, "Sorry. I tend to resort to sarcasm when I'm upset or uncomfortable or around other human beings."

He laughs. "Brennan's like that, too. I think he's funny. Andrews hates it, though."

"Yeah, well, Andrews hates most people and things."

"I've noticed that. I don't think he likes living in

Weltunkin at all. I think it was his wife's idea. You know, so she could be around family."

"Oh? I didn't know that."

"Before I worked those cases with you and Brennan, Andrews told me a few things. He doesn't really talk to me much anymore, though."

"That's because of exactly this. He's afraid you'll tell me and Mitchell what he said."

"Oh. I guess I really shouldn't be saying anything. Maybe he wanted it to be private."

"Maybe," I say. "I don't think you meant any harm, though."

"No. Definitely not." He pulls into the parking lot.

"What time does this place open? I can't believe there are so many cars here already." I thought people would at least wait until after dark to go somewhere like this so the entire town wouldn't see them.

"It opens at noon, actually, but it'll be dark soon anyway."

I look at the clock on the dashboard. Dad wasn't kidding when he said I was out cold for hours after that vision. "I should go in first on my own," I say. "We don't want anyone to know we're together."

"Sorry, Piper, but you're wrong there. I need to go in first so I'm already in position when you go inside. That way I can protect you the entire time you're in there." He cuts the engine. "Give me a five-minute head start."

I nod, which thankfully doesn't hurt anymore. I watch

him walk into the club. Then I check the clock on the dashboard and wait five minutes. It's probably the longest five minutes of my life. The second time is up, I open the car door and head for the entrance. The bass from inside the club greets me before I can even open the door. I have a feeling this is going to be sensory overload, something I should have taken into account before I even got out of the car. I need to center myself, but it's too late for that now.

I go inside and am greeted by a hostess, which I find a little surprising, but seeing as I've never been in a place like this before, I have no idea if that's normal. "Table for one?" the scantily clad woman asks me.

"Um, no. I'm actually here to ask about a job."

She steps around the hostess stand and looks me up and down. "Okay. You might work. Follow me." She waves me on, turns on a black stiletto, and walks down a hall in the opposite direction from the performers. I try to catch a glimpse of Officer Gilbert, but he must be blending in so well I can't pick him out. She brings me to a door, which I assume is an office, and knocks.

"Come in," says a voice from the other side of the door.

She opens it and says, "TJ, this woman wants to apply for a job."

TJ has curly black hair and a lot of freckles. His eyes roam over my body, making me feel extremely self-conscious and totally grossed out. His energy is...slimy. Mitchell would be introducing his fist to this guy's face for the thoughts that are most likely going through TJ's head right now. "Come on in, sugar. Take a seat." He looks up at the hostess. "Thanks, Suzie."

"Anytime, doll." She blows him a kiss and walks out.

I feel like I've entered an alternate universe or something. I sit down in the chair across from TJ.

"What's your name, love?"

"Becky," I say, blurting out the first name that pops into my mind, which also happens to be the name of that bimbo from the gym.

"And you want to be a dancer here, Becky? Do you have any experience?"

"Well, I work at a gym to keep myself fit. I teach a few aerobics classes there as well." I twirl the end of my hair around one finger. Totally stereotypical, but I'm completely at a loss for how to act.

The door behind me opens, and someone says, "TJ, I have those numbers for you."

I recognize the voice immediately. My luck could not be any worse.

"Becky, come meet another Becky," TJ says. "She's looking to dance here. She works at a gym like you, too."

Becky walks around the chairs to look at me head-on. She practically snarls when she says, "Her name's not Becky, and she most certainly does not work at a gym." She crosses her arms. "First you're snooping around at the gym and now here. What are you, a cop?"

So much for being undercover.

CHAPTER FIFTEEN

TJ stands up. "Who the hell are you, and why are you pretending to be someone you're not?"

Instead of answering TJ, I turn to Becky. "I'm here because of Mitchell."

She crosses her arms. "I've never seen him here."

I almost want to hug her for saying that. "I'm glad to hear it, but that's not what I meant. He's missing."

"What makes you think he'd be here?" she asks me.

I'm not ready to play the psychic card just yet, so I say, "He's a police detective. He's working a case that might have brought him here."

"Everything here is on the up-and-up," TJ says, reaching for the papers in Becky's hand. "My numbers are right here, and you'll see they match what I report to the IRS." He nods toward the door. "Thank you, Becky. You can go."

She doesn't look happy to be dismissed, but she doesn't protest either. She glares at me one last time before walking out of the office.

"I'm not talking about your books. Someone assaulted Mitchell sometime last night, I believe they might be holding him and another police officer in the basement of this club."

"Are you accusing one of my employees of something?" TJ tosses the papers on his desk and glares at me.

"I'm sure it's just a big misunderstanding. If you'll take me to the basement, we can clear all of this right up."

"Fine." TJ walks around the desk and motions for me to leave the office first.

I know I should go find Officer Gilbert to go with me, but TJ is actually willing to take me to the basement and I don't want him to change his mind. Of course, he might be willing to bring me down there because he plans to knock me out and tie me up as well.

My senses aren't going haywire, so I assume I'm not in any immediate danger. Once we're in the hallway again, TJ steps around me to lead the way. This time the door I'm brought to leads to a stairwell.

"Do you know all of your employees pretty well?" I ask as we start to descend the stairs.

"As well as an employer can, I suppose. Why do you ask?"

I want to say because I think someone is running an

illegal gambling ring in the basement of the club, but I refrain from disclosing that bit of information. "Everyone just seems pretty tight-knit."

"Happy employees are good employees."

"Agreed."

We reach the bottom of the stairs, and he flips a light switch. I immediately notice the floor is carpeted, and the walls don't have any wood paneling. This isn't the place I saw in my vision.

"Is this the only room in the basement?" I ask.

"Look around. What you see is what you get. This is just a storage area. There are no hidden rooms or anything. Like I said upstairs, I have nothing to hide. My business is all by the book."

My senses say he's telling the truth. "Maybe you can help me with something. I'm looking for somewhere that has a cement floor and wood paneling."

TJ laughs. "Did you assume this club had a 1970s' vibe?"

I bob my shoulders. "I've never been in here before. I thought it might be possible."

"I see. Well, I'm sorry to disappoint you, but as you can see, this isn't that place."

"But do you know anywhere that might fit that description?" I press.

To his credit, he takes a moment to consider it. "Sorry, but I can't think of anywhere."

"Well, then I guess I've taken up enough of your time.

Thank you for your help." I start up the stairs again.

"I'm not sure I did help, but you're welcome. And if you ever change your mind about dancing, you let me know."

I laugh. "Sorry, TJ, but I'm no Becky."

"Fair enough. But for the record, Becky has never danced here. She's my bookkeeper, and a damn good one at that. Don't judge her on her appearance alone. She's smart."

"Fair enough," I say, using his words.

He leads me out of the club, maybe because he doesn't trust that I won't stick around to snoop some more. I have no reason to. Mitchell isn't here. I don't know where he is. I call Dad and fill him in, and a few seconds later, he pulls up next to me in his BMW.

Officer Gilbert comes outside, looking a little too happy. "Hey, where did you go?"

"Where did *you* go?" I ask him.

"Nowhere. I swear." He holds up his hands. "I was sitting at a table. I saw you come in, but then you disappeared. I went toward the restrooms and looked around for you, but I couldn't find you."

"You were supposed to be watching out for her," Dad says, ducking down to glare at Officer Gilbert through the open passenger door.

"I tried."

"It's fine, Dad. I'm okay, and Mitchell isn't here. This was a dead end."

"Where are you off to next?" Officer Gilbert asks.

"I think I need another vision. We'll head back to Mitchell's place. Will you fill in the chief for us?"

"Sure thing. Let me know if you need my assistance again," Officer Gilbert says.

I give him a nod and get into the car. Dad drives off as soon as my seat belt is clicked. "So the basement checked out?"

"Yup. Carpet with painted walls." Now that I'm out of the club, the helplessness of the situation hits me hard. I lower my head and twist the ring on my pinky.

"Don't go there, pumpkin. We're going to find him, so stop thinking that we won't."

The problem isn't finding him. It's finding him before it's too late. "If Mitchell's in bad shape when I have this vision, it's going to put me out of commission for a while. Promise me you'll leave me and go search for him."

"Piper."

"No, Dad. You know the effects of my visions can't hurt me physically. The pain is psychological. I'll get over them and be fine. Mitchell won't be. You need to leave me to sleep it off and go find him. Promise me."

It takes him a moment to answer, but he finally gives in. "If that happens, I'll call your mother to come stay with you, and I'll go after Mitchell."

It's the best offer he's going to make, so I agree. "Okay, but call her on your way to Mitchell."

"Agreed."

Since the photograph is what showed me Mitchell's location, Dad and I go directly to the bedroom so I can read it again. This time, he makes me sit on the bed in case Mitchell gets knocked out again. Falling and hitting my head because of a vision is one way they can actually hurt me for real.

Dad puts a hand on my back for support as I center myself and prepare for the vision. When I'm ready, I close my eyes and place the photograph in my right hand.

A body lies faceup on the concrete floor, the face vaguely familiar.

"That's what you get for not cooperating, Cole. We had a good thing going here until you ruined it."

The vision ends, leaving me in utter confusion.

"What happened?"

"It doesn't make sense. I didn't see Mitchell. I saw Cole Bailey, and I think I've seen him before."

Dad repositions himself on the bed to face me. "What do you mean?"

"I think I saw him at Marcia's Nook one day. He was waiting to buy a book, and Marcia and I were so caught up talking that he had to say 'Excuse me' to get our attention."

"Have you seen him anywhere else?"

"No, I don't think so."

"Okay, but why would this photograph of you and Mitchell show you a vision of Cole Bailey?"

"I think maybe I was seeing what Mitchell was seeing. The killer's back was to Mitchell, so I didn't see his face. I heard him, though. He told Cole's dead body that this was for not cooperating. He said they had a good thing going."

"Do you think Cole was in on it? Like he was getting information from people at the gym and feeding it to this guy?"

No. "Uh-uh. My senses say no." I've felt all along that Cole was a good guy. He was even polite that day at Marcia's Nook even though I was holding up the line on him. I'm missing something. "Cole's the clue I need to figure out. He has to be."

"What about the surroundings?" Dad asks. "Could you tell where they are?"

"It was pretty dark. Not much lighting."

"So still most likely a basement."

"I'm going to try again."

"Piper, I think that's enough for today. It's late. We can't exactly go searching every basement in Weltunkin at night. Besides, Jez needs you."

Mitchell needs me. "Dad, will you pick up Jez and bring her to your place?"

"I know what you're thinking, and I don't think staying here is a good idea." He knows I'll keep trying to have visions until I get something useful.

"If I figure anything out, I'll call you immediately. I promise."

"I think I liked it better when you didn't date," he says before kissing my forehead.

I give him a weak smile. "I think I did, too." Heartache

is something I had only ever experienced through other people in visions. Feeling it firsthand is almost unbearable.

"I'll keep my phone with me. Call me if you need anything. I don't care what time it is."

"I will. Tell Jez I love her."

He nods and walks out.

I stare at Mitchell's image in the picture. "Where are you? Why won't you show me? You should know I'd try to find you, and you should give me a clue. Come on, Mitchell. You claim to know me so well. Figure out what I'm doing, and do something that will show me where you are!" I'm yelling at his image now.

Tears spill down my face, dotting the glass and frame. I wipe them away and crawl into Mitchell's bed. I fall asleep hugging the photograph to me and breathing in his scent on the sheets.

The room is mostly dark. Barely any sunlight is coming through one small window near the ceiling. Three bodies are lying on the floor. One is upside down. The other two are face-up. Officer Andrews's gaze is vacant, and a trickle of blood seeps from the bullet wound in his forehead. Beside him is Mitchell. His eyes glazed and the same bullet wound between his eyes.

I bolt upright and drop the photograph into my lap. I'm shaking so hard the bed is creaking from the movement. I reach a finger toward Mitchell's image. "Don't do this to me. You can't make me love you and then leave me. Mitchell, please!"

CHAPTER SIXTEEN

My phone rings, and I scramble for my purse at the foot of the bed. It's Chief Johansen. "Chief?" I answer.

"Ashwell, sorry for the early call, but we have a possible break in the case, and I figured you'd want to know."

"What is it?"

"We've managed to get the name of the bookie. You were right about it being the grandson of the woman the phone number is registered to. His name is Isaiah Young. We had trouble finding him at first because he has a different last name than everyone else in his family. It made it difficult to make the connection. Apparently, his mother gave him his father's last name even though his mother never married him."

I really don't care about Isaiah's family history. I just

want to know where to find this guy. "Do you have an address?"

"I'm sending Officer Wallace to you now."

"I'm at Mitchell's place. I stayed here so I could read some more of his things."

"Okay, I'll redirect Wallace. Harry will be with him. He has Mitchell's scent, so if he's at Young's place, Harry will know."

That's good. "Thank you, Chief."

"Ashwell, have you had any more visions? Is there anything I should know?"

I swallow hard. "One woke me up right before you called."

"Are you sure it was a vision?"

"Yes, this time I could tell."

"Okay. What did you see?"

"Cole Bailey is dead already, and Mitchell and Officer Andrews will be too if we don't find them soon."

"I'm calling Wallace now. Expect him in ten minutes." He ends the call.

I give myself exactly thirty seconds to fall apart, and then I get out of bed, pull off the stupid dress I wore to the strip club, and rifle through Mitchell's closet for something that won't look absolutely ridiculous on me. I settle on a button-down shirt that comes well past my butt. It's a good thing Mitchell has a good six inches on me. I grab a belt and hope I can pass this shirt off as a dress.

Officer Wallace pulls up out front just as I'm grabbing

my purse and getting off the phone with Dad. He's going to text Officer Wallace for the address and meet us at Isaiah Young's place.

"Good morning," Officer Wallace says. He eyes my outfit. "Is that new?"

"To me, yes. It's Mitchell's. I didn't have any clothes to wear after my undercover operation last night with Officer Gilbert."

Officer Wallace backs out of the driveway. "I heard about that. I'm sorry I missed you in disguise." He laughs. "I have to be honest. I just can't picture it. Officer Gilbert says you pulled it off, though."

"Can we never speak of it again, please? I really don't want Mitchell to find out about it."

"Sorry, Piper, but everyone at the station knows. There's no way Mitchell won't hear about it."

Yes, there is. If we don't find him, he won't be alive to hear about my utter humiliation.

Officer Wallace must sense my despair because he motions to the back seat. "Harry is resting up. He'll be good to go when we get there."

I peek over my shoulder at the sleeping K9. "Sorry to get you both out of bed so early on a Sunday."

"*You* didn't. The WPD doesn't take lightly to people kidnapping our men."

"So I've heard."

"I've already heard you don't take it lightly either. How are you holding up?"

I look down at my purse in my lap. "I brought this along." I pull out the photograph of Mitchell and me, sans frame. "I've been using it to spark visions of where he is. I thought it might be useful to bring with us in case this turns out to be another dead end."

"You don't think it's the bookie." It's not a question, but I answer anyway.

"No, I don't. I feel strongly that Cole Bailey is the key to unraveling all of this. He worked out at the same gym Austin Hawkins and Officer Andrews did. He spotted them both, and I have a feeling he was friendly with them both, too. I can't help thinking they told him about the bets and that led to not only Austin's death but Cole's as well."

"Sorry, Piper, but what you just said makes it seem like the bookie is the best suspect."

I sigh. "I know it seems that way, but it's not right. I can't explain how I know that. I just do."

"You don't have to explain anything to me. I've seen you in action. I know I'm not the biggest believer in what you do, but I've never seen you be wrong. I can't explain how you solve these cases or how you know things. I just know you do." He shakes his head. "I'm not explaining it well."

"No, you're doing fine. Most people can't wrap their heads around what I do. Hell, some days I can't either. But you've never dismissed one of my visions, and for that I'm very grateful. I mean, you even congratulated me when I had my first premonition."

"To be honest, I wasn't sure how I was supposed to react, so I hope that was okay."

I laugh. "Anything is better than Officer Andrews's reaction to my abilities."

"And yet, here you are, trying to save his life, too."

"I'm sure you've saved people who weren't exactly nice to you," I say.

He meets my gaze briefly. "My first year on the force, I stopped a jumper. He wasn't happy with me at all. In fact, he called me every name you could imagine. He hated me for not letting him jump."

"But you did the right thing," I say.

"I know. If I had the opportunity to do it all over, I'd save him again." He smiles. "He gave me a black eye, though."

"Really?"

"Yup. I had to charge him with assaulting a police officer. Then he really hated me."

I laugh, and it feels good. "Thank you. I know you told me that to make me feel better and to get my mind off Mitchell. It worked on both counts."

He smiles and pulls up to an old house on the same road Austin Hawkins lived on.

"Whoa," I say.

"What? Are you sensing something?" He cuts the engine and looks at me.

"No. It's just that I've been on this road. Two houses over, in fact. No wonder Austin had a mirror on him. He lived two houses over from the bookie he thought was coming after him for money."

"Do you think he knew?" Officer Wallace asks me. "I mean the bookie goes by Ebenezer. No one would connect that name to Isaiah Young."

No, they wouldn't. "I don't know if he had any idea it was him or if he even knew his neighbors at all."

"Small world, huh?"

"Small town," I say, opening the car door.

Officer Wallace opens the back door, and Harry jumps out, now fully awake. I realize he probably wasn't sleeping at all on the way here. He was most likely preparing himself, kind of like the way I prepare myself before a vision.

"Ready?" Officer Wallace asks me.

"Ready."

Officer Wallace gives Harry a bandana to sniff, and even though I'm not a K9, I can sense Mitchell's energy coming off it. Once Harry is ready, we start toward the front door.

A thought strikes me and doesn't exactly put me at ease. "Hey, are you planning to bust him for illegal gambling?"

"Not at this moment. This is about finding Mitchell and Andrews. If they're here, the gambling charges will pale in comparison to abducting two police officers."

Not to mention killing Cole Bailey. But again, I don't think Isaiah Young did either of those things. I'm not convinced he doesn't know who did, though, so this is worth looking into.

Officer Wallace rings the doorbell of the old Victorian home. It takes several minutes and another two rings of the bell for someone to answer, most likely because they were asleep.

"Can I help you?" the man asks, followed by a yawn.

"Are you Isaiah Young?" Officer Wallace asks.

"Who's asking?" Isaiah seems more awake now that he's been identified by name.

"I'm Officer Wallace with the Weltunkin PD, and this is Piper Ashwell, a private investigator who works closely with the WPD."

"And the dog?" Isaiah asks.

"That's Harry," I say.

"What's this about?" Isaiah asks, still not confirming his identity.

"Two police officers have gone missing, and we're asking local residents if they've seen them. Harry here is along to try to pick up on their scents." Officer Wallace holds up two photographs. "Have you seen either of these police officers?"

Isaiah looks at the pictures for about two seconds before saying, "Nope. Sorry." He starts to shut the door.

"Before you go, I have another question for you, Ebenezer," I say.

He pauses but keeps a straight face. "Don't know anyone by that name."

"Really? I find that odd because this officer,"—I take Officer Andrews's picture from Officer Wallace—"Officer Kurt Andrews, has been helping to keep your name off the police radar. You know him, don't you, Ebenezer?"

Isaiah starts to shut the door again, but Officer Wallace says, "If you don't want to go to prison for countless years, I suggest you cooperate with our investigation."

"He's right, you know." I put my left hand on the door. "I should mention I happen to be psychic. I can tell you that cooperating with the police will significantly reduce your punishment." I soften my tone. "Look, we just want to find these two officers of the law. Right now, I couldn't care less about some bets, and I don't think Officer Wallace does either. Help us find them, and Officer Andrews won't be the only cop doing you some favors."

I can tell Officer Wallace isn't happy about the promises I'm making, but I'm going to say whatever I need to find Mitchell.

Isaiah looks past us and then motions us inside.

Harry leads the way, and I'm pretty sure he's trained to do that. Isaiah brings us into the kitchen, which is tiny and has a mustard yellow refrigerator. He's smart not to flaunt the money I'm sure he has. This place is seriously stuck several decades in the past, which makes me wonder if the basement could have wood paneling after all. Maybe my senses have been really off where Isaiah is concerned.

"The truth is I heard about Hawkins getting shot in

the head. Andrews called me and assured me he was taking care of it and my name would stay out of the case."

"I'm aware," I say, and I decide to take a big leap of faith. "I'm also aware that you didn't kill Hawkins."

He bobs his head. "Of course, I didn't. The guy was a hothead. Sure, he won big, but I know his type. In one week's time, he would've been betting those winnings and losing again. I wasn't worried about him."

My senses are telling me he's being honest.

"When was the last time you spoke to or saw Kurt Andrews?" Officer Wallace asks.

"It's been a few days."

"What about the other man? Detective Brennan?" I ask. "Have you even seen him before?"

Isaiah shakes his head. "Nah. Never seen him."

"He spoke to you on the phone. He placed a bet under the name Bob. Do you remember? You thought it was funny that he called himself Bob after you told him to call you Ebenezer."

Isaiah nods. "Yeah, I remember that. He won his bet. Tiny payout. I called him up Friday night to let him know. I thought it was odd that instead of wanting to use his winnings to place a new bet, he said he wanted to cash out. I told him I'd meet up with him Monday to take care of it."

Officer Wallace looks at me, most likely trying to judge if I think Isaiah is telling the truth or not. He is. And I know Mitchell planned to meet him so he could do exactly what we're doing now, getting information out of him.

"What about Cole Bailey? Do you know him?"

"No. Not that many of my clients give me their real names. Most like to keep things confidential."

"How did you find out Andrews was a cop then?" I ask.

"Easy. His picture was in the paper. I knew what he looked like from our transactions. I called him out on it, and he offered me some protection." He scoffs. "A lot of good that did me."

"I'm going to level with you. Four men are missing or dead. Three of them have placed bets with you. Two have won big money. The connection between them seems to be Cole Bailey."

"Like I said, I don't know anyone who goes by that name." He grips the back of a kitchen chair.

"I believe you. Can you tell me where you were supposed to meet Mitchell—I mean Bob on Monday morning?"

"Why? You think someone tapped my phone line or something and was offing these guys to steal their money?"

Officer Wallace's eyes widen. "That might be worth looking into. This person was certainly getting information from somewhere, and that would explain it."

"No," I say, immediately sensing that's wrong. "But you are right about them getting information about the bets. The killer absolutely was. Just not through Isaiah."

"Does that mean I'm in the clear?" he asks.

"Afraid not," Officer Wallace says. "We've got enough

to arrest you, but I will make sure your cooperation in this case is known." He pulls out his handcuffs and reads Isaiah his rights.

"You've got to be kidding me. I even invited you into my home." His gaze falls on me. "And you, you said cooperating would help me. You..." His eyes narrow on me. "Wait a second. You're the lady Andrews warned me about, aren't you? He said he'd keep you away from me."

"Yeah, that's me. He actually tried to pin the murders on me to clear your name, so he kept his word. The problem is he got himself abducted, and now he might die because of you."

"I want my lawyer. I'm not confessing to anything."

I don't bother telling him he already confessed to a whole lot.

Officer Wallace calls for backup since we have Harry to bring to the station and he doesn't trust Isaiah in the back seat with Harry. I can't blame him either. Officer Gilbert shows up and takes care of Isaiah for us.

"I should follow them," Officer Wallace says as Dad pulls up in his BMW.

"Go ahead. I'll catch a ride with my dad."

He nods and gets Harry into the car.

Dad gets out of his car and hurries over to me. "Sorry I'm so late. There was an accident, and the road was closed. They weren't letting anyone through."

"That's okay. Officer Wallace arrested Isaiah Young

for the illegal gambling ring. Mitchell and Andrews aren't here, though."

Dad eyes me. "I can see the wheels turning in your head. Did you figure something out?"

"Maybe. It was actually something Isaiah said. Someone was getting information about the bets, but they weren't getting it from Isaiah."

"So where was the information coming from?"

"That's the key, isn't it?" As soon as I say it, I realize what the answer is. "Cole Bailey is the key. I said that before."

"Slow down, pumpkin. I think I missed something along the way."

"The killer was getting information from Cole Bailey. Only Cole didn't realize what he was doing. He's just a chatty person. People opened up to him because he's easy to talk to. He found out about the bets at the gym, and I'm willing to bet he told someone else without thinking twice about it."

"Someone like who?"

"The killer."

"Yes, but who is the killer, Piper?"

"Someone he'd talk to on a regular basis. That's the only way they'd know about the bets in a timely manner."

"A family member?"

No. "Uh-uh, that feels wrong to me."

"A friend?"

"I'm not getting a yes or no on that. Hmm."

"Who else would he be in contact with on a regular basis who may or may not be a friend?" Dad asks, looking at the Victorian house.

I follow his gaze, and the answer comes to me immediately. "A roommate."

CHAPTER SEVENTEEN

I grab Dad's arm. "It's Cole's roommate. The basement must be in the house they both share. Dad, this is it. We have him!"

"Piper, slow down. Remember how much trouble we had trying to find Cole online?"

"You said he lived in Weltunkin. I thought that meant you had an address."

"No. His Facebook profile listed Weltunkin as his hometown. That's all."

"Then we need to get digging because that's where we'll find Mitchell and Officer Andrews. I know it."

Dad nods. "Let's go to the office and get to work."

We rush to the car, and while he drives, I call Chief Johansen. "Chief, it's Piper Ashwell."

"Wallace just got here with Isaiah Young. Nice work."

"I have better news, but I need your help. I think the person who has Mitchell and Officer Andrews is Cole Bailey's roommate."

"What's the name?"

"I don't have one, and I don't have an address for Bailey either. That's what I need you to find for me."

"Cole Bailey. Got it. I'll run it through the system and see what comes up. Ashwell, are you sure this is our guy?"

"Positive." I tell him how I reached the conclusion.

"I'm a little surprised you didn't figure this out through other means."

"You forget I'm a licensed private investigator. I'm pretty good at figuring things out with just my deductive reasoning skills as well."

"I see that now. Good work, Ashwell. I'll be in touch." He ends the call.

"He's on it," I tell Dad.

He reaches for my left hand and squeezes it. "We're going to find them in time."

"I hope so." I pull the photograph out of my purse and stare at Mitchell's image. I can't just sit around, hoping the chief or our search yields an address for Bailey. I need to be more proactive. "Dad, change of plans. We need to go to the gym near my office. Bailey has a membership there, which means his address must be on file."

Dad nods. "You got it. You know they aren't going to turn that information over to you, right?"

I know. I'm going to have to beg Becky to bend some rules and help me on Mitchell's behalf, and if that doesn't work, I'm going to have to get the information I need through more creative means.

Luckily, the gym is open seven days a week. I spot Becky behind the desk when we walk in. She looks up, and immediately, her eyes narrow on me.

"We reserve the right to deny membership to anyone we don't deem trustworthy, and seeing as you tried to pretend you were me, I don't think we could trust any information you'd provide on the membership application. Sorry." She grabs her clipboard and starts to walk away.

"Wait. About that. I'm sorry. The truth is I'm a private investigator working with the Weltunkin PD on a case. Two men, who were both members of this gym, are already dead. Two others are missing. One is the man we were with the other day. Mitchell. Do you remember him?" I ask.

Becky turns around, the clipboard clutched to her chest. "You mean the man that hit on me? The man who is supposedly your boyfriend?" Her voice is laced with sarcasm.

I nod. "I'm sorry about that, but sometimes cases call for desperate measures. Mitchell is one of the missing men I just mentioned. He was working undercover, and no one has seen him since Friday night."

She laughs. "He's probably with some woman. I know

men like him. The 'love 'em and leave 'em' type. Sorry to tell you this, but you've been ditched, honey."

I take a deep breath and let it all out. "I'm going to level with you. That was Mitchell once upon a time. It's not him anymore."

She laughs again. "Tell me you aren't the pathetic type who believes she can change a man."

"Not at all. But that doesn't mean I don't believe people can change on their own. You want to know the truth? Who I really am? I'm psychic. I had a vision of Mitchell being held hostage. I thought it was in the basement of the club where you work, but I was wrong. He's at Cole Bailey's house."

"Cole?" She flinches and shakes her head. "No way. He's like the nicest guy. Practically everyone here knows him. He's never hurt anyone."

"He didn't. His roommate did. And I also had a vision of his roommate killing Cole."

She brings her hand to her mouth in horror. "Look, I'm not saying I believe in psychics, but if that's true..." She bites her lower lip. "I always hoped Cole would ask me out. He seemed like a really decent person. It's tough to find people like that nowadays. Especially here. Everyone's a hothead, thinking big muscles will make them better than everyone else."

"What about Austin Hawkins?" Dad asks, speaking for the first time since we got here.

"Austin." She pauses as if trying to place the name to a face. "Oh, yeah. I remember him. He was trying to bulk up. He looked kind of paranoid. I remember he never went out into the parking lot without looking through the window first."

"That's because he knew someone was after him."

"Is he...the other man you mentioned who died?"

I nod. "He was shot in the head in his car in his very own driveway."

She brings her hand to her mouth again. "That's horrible."

"Becky, I know this breaks every rule in the book, but I need to know where Cole Bailey lived. That's where I'm going to find Mitchell and the other officer who was abducted. If I don't get to them soon, they're both going to die like Cole and Austin did."

"My boss will kill me. I'll lose my job. I have a kid to raise, you know."

I never saw her being a single mother. It explains why she's working two jobs, though. "I'll make you a deal. If he finds out I got the address from your records, I'll swear that I came by the information through a psychic vision. I won't tell a soul that you gave it to me."

"There are cameras in this place." She doesn't move her head, but her eyes jut upward toward the corner to her left. It's aimed at the door. When she gave Mitchell that list, she must have made it look like she was handing him paperwork for his membership or even her phone number if they were flirting.

"Are there any blind spots? Places the camera doesn't reach?" Dad asks.

Becky shrugs. "I wouldn't know. I've never viewed the footage."

Damn it. "Okay, what if you tell me where this information is?"

"It's in our computer system."

I look at the desk. There's no way to discreetly touch the computer without the camera catching me in the act, and I can't think of a reason to touch the computer without looking suspicious to anyone who views the footage.

"Can you look up the information and text it to me?" I ask.

"I'd need a reason to go into the client files. It's private information. My boss can see when anyone accesses it. Searching information beyond a simple name will raise my boss's eyebrow."

I rack my brain, trying to come up with a solution. "What if you say I came in because the police suspect Cole Bailey is missing, and you wanted to try calling him to follow up, so you accessed his file to do so?"

"I guess that would be okay. But I don't think you should be here when I do it. It would look too suspicious."

I nod. "We'll leave. Wait a minute or two, and then look up the address. Then call Cole's number so your story will check out if anyone asks. After that, text me his address." I jot my number on a gym brochure.

"I can do that." She walks back behind her desk.

"Thank you, Becky. I really appreciate this."

Tears fill her eyes. "I hope you find them. There aren't a lot of nice guys left in this town. We can't afford to lose any more."

Even without reading her, I know the father of her child isn't alive. "I'm sorry for your loss."

She offers me a weak smile. "Thanks. I hate that my baby will never know her daddy. She's here, you know. In the daycare center. I get an employee discount, and I get to pop in and see her throughout the day. My mom watches her in the evenings while I'm at the club. I'll have to quit that job before my daughter is old enough to know what a strip club is."

"Why? You're their bookkeeper, right? There's no shame in that." I reach forward and place my left hand on hers. "I'm sure your daughter would be very proud of you for doing everything in your power to give her a good life. You're a great mom."

She wipes a tear from her eye. "Thank you."

I offer her one last smile before Dad and I leave.

He puts his arm around me. "You're getting a lot better with people, pumpkin."

No doubt from hanging around with Mitchell. I need to get him back.

"Hey." Dad pulls me closer to his side as we walk. "In

a few minutes, we'll have the address, and then we'll bring him home." He always could read my mind.

I hold my phone in my hand as we sit in the car and wait for Becky's text. It feels like it takes forever, and when my phone chimes with the notification, I actually jump.

"This is it," I tell Dad as I open the message.

"1412 Montgomery Street," I say, and Dad puts the address into his navigation system.

While he drives, I call Chief Johansen.

"Ashwell, I was just about to call you. There's no address in the system for Cole Bailey. He doesn't even have a driver's license on record. I'm assuming he either just moved or his name isn't really Cole Bailey."

"He just moved. Someone at the gym mentioned that." It also explains why he didn't know his roommate was a lowlife thief, abductor, and murderer. "I'm guessing the house belongs to the roommate, and Bailey moved in because he's new to town, needed a place to live, and was looking to split the cost of rent."

"So what's your next move then?" the chief asks.

"I have the address. That's why I called you."

"Should I ask how you got this information?"

"It's probably better that you don't," I say. Mitchell is used to looking the other way when I bend the rules, but I'm not sure the chief will be as willing, and I also don't want to get Becky into any trouble. She's really growing on me now that I know her story.

"Dad and I are on our way there now. It's 1412 Montgomery Street."

"I'll send Wallace. I don't want you two going in there unarmed. Hang back and wait for Wallace. Do you understand?"

Sit back and wait while Mitchell could be held at gunpoint? I don't think so. "Sorry, Chief, reception is terrible here. I can't hear you." I end the call and look at Dad, who is eyeing me.

"He told us to wait for an officer, didn't he?" Dad asks.

I shrug. "Not sure. I couldn't hear him." I don't want Dad getting into hot water because of me, so it's best not to be forthright with him at the moment, even if he can tell I'm lying through my teeth.

He shakes his head and keeps driving. We don't pull up to the house. Instead, Dad parks down the street, three houses away. "It's the red brick raised ranch," he tells me, even though I can figure that out on my own since every house on the street has a number on a green sign sticking in the grass at the edge of the property.

"We know they're in the basement, so we should head around to the back of the house and look for an entry."

Dad motions to my purse. "Try reading the photo again. See if you can spot a door or any way to the outside."

I pull the photo from my purse and swallow hard. I close my eyes and focus on Mitchell.

He's sitting on the cement floor, his hands cuffed

behind him. Officer Andrews is slumped over beside him. Mitchell looks around the room. Cole Bailey's lifeless body is lying in the center of it. Light is coming from the small window near the ceiling.

"I'm not seeing a door anywhere," I tell Dad when the vision ends. "And I'm not sure if Officer Andrews is still alive. In my previous vision he was lying on the ground. This time he was slumped over."

"So either he fell asleep, or things changed from the last time you had a vision."

That's the problem with premonitions. They don't always come to be the way they are in visions. Things can change, which changes the future.

"I only saw a small window on the one wall. I'm not even sure it opens."

"That means the only way into the basement is through the house itself," Dad says. "We're going to have to wait for Wallace."

The problem is, I'm not sure if I just saw Mitchell in real time. It's possible what I saw already happened. It felt pretty immediate, but that doesn't mean it didn't happen moments earlier. "We can't wait. We need to get in there now."

"Pumpkin, if this guy sees us lurking, he might kill Mitchell and Andrews," Dad says. "We can't risk it."

"If he sees the police at his door, he'll probably kill either Mitchell or Andrews and use the other as a human shield to get out of the house. We have a better chance of sneaking up on him than Officer Wallace does." I open the car door, not willing to sit here and debate this. Officer Wallace is already on his way. I have to move before he gets here.

Dad follows me. "At least stay behind me," he says.

I don't point out that we know this guy is armed. It would take two shots to take us both out. Which one of us is shot first doesn't really make a difference. Instead, I let Dad play the role of protector and lead the way. He brings us through the backyard of the neighboring house. It doesn't appear that anyone is home here. There are no cars in the driveway and no lights on in the house. We creep through their backyard to the other side of the house closest to the brick raised ranch.

Dad stops, and I know he's trying to look for signs of life in the house. There's only one window on this side of the ranch, and the curtains are closed.

"Let's go," I say. "No one is watching."

There's a tree between the two yards, and Dad motions to it. It would be a good plan, making our way to the tree and then checking the window again, if not for the fact that it's slowing us down and allowing Officer Wallace time to get here. Dad pauses at the tree, but I keep going, staying low to the ground and ducking behind the house, out of sight of the window. I look back at Dad, who is still behind the tree. He shakes his head at me, but then his gaze rises to the window, and he steps back, fully concealing himself.

The killer must be in the window. That means I can get to the basement window without being seen. I make my move, still staying low to be on the safe side. At the window, I lie down in the grass and cup my hands around my eyes to peer inside. The basement looks exactly like it did in my vision. The wood paneling, the cement floor, Cole's body in the center of the room, and Mitchell against one wall. I smile when I see he's okay, and I feel a warm tear trek down my cheek.

He looks up, probably because I'm blocking the sunlight from coming through the window. His eyes widen when he sees me. Instead of being happy I'm here, he looks scared.

I hear a sliding glass door open to my right and know the killer is coming outside. I roll myself under the low deck and out of sight. There's just enough room for me to squeeze in, but I'm not completely out of view. If the killer looks down, he'll see my white dress shirt through the deck's floor beams. And if he steps off the deck, I'll be in full view.

I try to stay as still as possible. My pulse is pounding in my ears. Footsteps above me turn in my direction. I'm going to get caught. He must have heard me when I rolled under here. Or maybe he somehow saw me from the window. I'm not sure which, but he clearly knows someone is out here.

I have no weapon. Nothing at all to defend myself with. I'm a sitting duck as I listen to his footsteps descend the stairs. I can't believe this is how it's going to end. I just hope Officer Wallace gets here in time to save Mitchell.

I see the black boots coming toward me. I have seconds before I'm in the killer's view. I do the only thing I can. I close my eyes.

CHAPTER EIGHTEEN

"Good afternoon," I hear Dad yell. "I'm here to read your water meter."

I open my eyes to see Dad hurrying across the lawn.

"Sorry if I startled you," Dad says. "I admit it's kind of awkward walking through everyone's yards like this." Dad keeps his eyes on the killer's face, but with his hand, he discreetly waves two fingers, indicating I need to move. Now.

I quickly roll out from under the deck and up the stairs.

"I saw you from the window," the killer says.

So that's what brought him out here. He didn't hear or see me at all. He saw Dad behind the tree.

"Where's your meter reader?"

Oh God. Dad's going to be caught lying. I'm standing at the back door, not sure if I should sneak inside to rescue

Mitchell or stay out here to try to help Dad. The killer doesn't have his gun out, but I'm sure it's on him somewhere.

"Would you believe the darn thing broke?" Dad says. "Rotten luck, I swear. I have to read the meters the old-fashioned way today." He taps the side of his head, indicating his eyes.

"Where's your clipboard or notepad to write down the readings?" The killer obviously isn't satisfied, despite the fact that Dad's doing a pretty good job of improvising.

Dad whips out his phone. "Recording it all on here."

I slowly start to pull open the sliding glass door, which squeaks in the tracks much like it did when the killer came out here.

Dad clears his throat, I'm assuming to try to cover the sound. "Can you show me where your meter is? I'm new to this route, so I've been wandering through yards all day trying to locate everyone's meters."

I slip inside and shut the door behind me, hoping the killer didn't turn around in time to see me. I didn't see a water meter, which means they'll most likely have to walk past the back door to the other side of the house. That is if the killer believes Dad's story.

I move through the eat-in kitchen to a door I'm hoping leads to the basement. I try to turn the knob, but it's locked. Since I left my purse in the car, I don't have the lockpick kit on me, so I look around the kitchen for something to use on the lock. I settle on a steak knife.

Worst case scenario, I have a weapon now if the killer comes back inside. Of course, it won't do me much good against a gun aimed at my head.

I jimmy the tip of the knife in the lock. I'm sure Dad is doing his best to stall, but how much time can he really buy me when all he has to do is read a meter? I doubt the killer is the chatty type. He's more of a listener, which is how he targeted Hawkins and Andrews. I hear footsteps on the deck and have to abandon my attempt with the lock. I duck into the living room, looking for a place to hide. I settle for the space between the couch and the wall.

Someone knocks on the door, and I'm sure it's Officer Wallace. If I had my phone on me, I'd text him to tell him Mitchell is definitely here, but all I can do is stay crouched in my hiding spot and hope Officer Wallace can get this guy to invite him inside. He has no warrant and no probable cause since we don't know the killer's name and have no physical evidence to link him to any crime. The police don't even have proof that Cole Bailey is dead. They have nothing but what I've sensed.

The killer crosses the living room and pulls the curtain aside. "What the hell are the cops doing here?" he grumbles, and I duck down lower, hoping he doesn't spot me.

He opens the door but keeps a hand on it to deny entry. "Can I help you?"

"I hope so. I'm Officer Wallace with the Weltunkin PD. I'm following up on a reported missing person."

"What missing person?" the killer asks.

"Cole Bailey. One of his friends reported him missing. Apparently, he hasn't shown up at work or the gym in days, and none of his friends or family members have seen him."

"Sorry, but I don't know anyone by that name," the killer says. "How did you get this address?"

"Oh, this is the address Mr. Bailey gave his employer," Officer Wallace lies. "You're saying it's incorrect?"

"Yeah, that's what I'm saying. I live alone."

"I see. This is 1412 Montgomery Street, is it not?"

"Yeah."

"Hmm. I wonder why Mr. Bailey would list this as his address if he doesn't live here."

"Maybe he mixed up the numbers. Some people do that. Try 1214 Montgomery Street." Unfortunately, this guy is just as good at improvising as Officer Wallace.

"Good idea. I'll do that. Thank you for your time, Mr....?"

"Rogers," the killer says, and my senses tell me he's using a fake name.

"Mr. Rogers. Now there was a good neighbor," Officer Wallace jokes.

The killer forces one quick laugh. "Yeah. Well, good luck." He closes the door.

I have no idea what Officer Wallace's next move will be. Probably calling for backup. And where is my dad? The killer doesn't leave the living room. He watches out the front window, clearly waiting for Officer Wallace to leave.

I'm stranded. But there is something I can do. I can read the knife in my left hand and figure out who this guy is. Of course, I can't get that information to the police, so I'm not sure what help it will be.

Once the killer finally leaves the room, I switch the knife to my right hand and close my eyes.

The killer is sitting at the kitchen table counting stacks of hundred-dollar bills. "Easiest money I ever made." When he's finished, he puts the money into a duffle bag and carries it into another room.

If I find that bag, I'll have proof. The bills should be able to be traced back to Isaiah Young. Or maybe not since the bets were illegal in the first place. The killer is in the kitchen. I think. Though it's possible he went to the basement. I doubt he'll stick around this place after the police showed up at his front door. The question is, will he leave Mitchell and Officer Andrews, or will he kill them before taking off with the money?

I reach my senses out, trying to get a feel for the killer's mood. He's too far away, though, and I can't get a read on him. I decide to leave my hiding place. I slip along the wall to the edge of the couch and peer around it toward the kitchen. All I can make out is the sink and corner cabinet, so I still don't know if the killer is in the kitchen or if he went downstairs.

I slip out into the open and tiptoe across the room,

listening for any sounds from the kitchen. A chair slides across the kitchen floor, which means the killer is on the move. I make a split-second decision and race as quietly as possible into the nearest room, which happens to be a bedroom, and judging by the energy in here, I'm willing to bet this is where the killer sleeps.

I couldn't have chosen a worse room to hide in. The money must be in here somewhere, and I'm positive the killer will come for it so he can get out of here before Officer Wallace returns with backup.

I have two options, and they are both the most cliché hiding places of all time: the closet or under the bed. Worse, one of them is most likely the place where he stashed the duffel bag full of money. If I choose incorrectly, I'll be found the second the killer goes for the bag.

I decide on under the bed since I'm not positive there's enough room for me to hide in the closet and still be able to shut the door. The second I'm under the bed, I regret my decision. I have to cover my nose with my hand to stop myself from sneezing. The dust bunnies under here are bigger than Jezebel. The only good thing is I don't see the duffle bag.

The bedroom door is pushed fully open, and the same black boots from earlier appear as the killer walks to the closet, where I can see him in full view. He opens the door and grabs the duffle bag. He takes a few items of clothing and shoves them on top of the money inside the bag. I'm assuming he wants it to appear like he just has clothing in the bag if anyone sees him open it.

Then he pulls up the bottom of his shirt to reveal the gun in the waistband of his jeans. He checks the chamber to see how many bullets are inside and then closes it. "Time to tie up the loose ends."

He's going to kill Mitchell and Officer Andrews. A plan forms in my head. A totally crazy plan. Not as crazy as trying to jump the guy from behind and wrestle the gun out of his hand, but still crazy enough to get me killed.

I wait until he leaves the room before sliding out from under the bed. I peek my head out of the room to see him turning into the kitchen. Taking a deep breath, I slip the knife through the inside loop on my belt buckle to conceal it, leave the room, and start for the front door. I pull the door open, spin around to make it look like I just walked in, and yell, "Baby, are you home?"

It takes all of five seconds before the killer enters the living room, completely red-faced and gun trained at my head.

CHAPTER NINETEEN

"Oh," I say, putting my hand to my chest. "Sorry to startle you. You must be Cole's roommate. I'm Becky." I hold out my hand, which is shaking.

The killer doesn't move. "Close the door behind you," he orders.

"Right. Sorry about that." I turn around and catch a glimpse of Dad out front. He looks horrified as I close the door. "Is this a bad neighborhood?" I ask. "Cole never mentioned anything about crime here, but you never can be too careful these days, can you? Personally, I think everyone should carry a gun to protect themselves." I'm rambling, but hopefully he's buying my ruse.

When I face him again, the gun is still aimed at me. "You can lower that now. I already told you who I am, though I guess I should mention I'm Cole's girlfriend. He left his key at my place. I'm just returning it."

The killer dips his head toward the coffee table. "Leave it there. Cole isn't here."

"Oh, well I guess I'll just hold on to the key and give it to him when I see him later."

"No. Leave it. This is my place, and I don't really like the idea of people having keys so they can come and go as they please."

I don't have a key on me. Not even my own since I don't have my purse. "Look, I don't know you and you don't know me. I'd really rather give the key directly back to Cole, if you don't mind."

"I do mind. Like I said, this is *my* place. He's just renting a room from me."

"I get it. Maybe I can wait here for him." That might keep him from killing Mitchell and Officer Andrews. He could just make a run for it with the money, and hopefully Officer Wallace will be outside ready to grab him. I start for the couch.

"I don't have time to entertain houseguests," he says. "Leave the key and get out."

Another knock sounds on the door, and the killer and I both turn toward it.

"Someone with you?" he asks me.

I shake my head.

"Why do I feel like you're lying?"

"I swear I'm not."

The knock comes again, and this time Officer Wallace says, "WPD! Open up!"

Damn it! The killer grabs my arm before I can even blink. "Let's go. You're my ticket out of this place."

I know it's stupid, but I have no other ideas, so I yell, "Come on in! It's open!" Thank God I didn't lock the door.

Officer Wallace, now with permission to enter, barges right in with his gun drawn.

"That wasn't smart," the killer growls in my ear, pulling my body in front of him and aiming the gun at my head.

"Don't move," Officer Wallace yells.

Officer Gilbert and Dad are behind him. Officer Gilbert has his gun raised as well, but neither can take a shot since I'm the only open target at the moment.

"Drop your weapons, or I will blow her head off," the killer says.

I meet Dad's gaze, and I give him a brave smile. "Tell Mitchell I love him."

"Tell him yourself," he says, and his eyes lower to my side where the knife I tucked into Mitchell's belt is now slightly exposed.

I reach for it very slowly so the killer doesn't sense what I'm doing.

"I mean it. Drop your weapons, or I *will* kill her."

I grip the handle of my knife in my left hand, count to three, and then plunge the blade into the killer's thigh.

He yells and releases his grip on me. I drop to the floor

out of his reach, giving Officer Wallace a clear shot. But he doesn't shoot.

"Drop the weapon!" Officer Wallace shouts.

Instead of dropping the gun, the guy fires several shots. I cover my head. When I look up, the killer is gone. Officer Wallace, Officer Gilbert, and Dad all scramble back onto their feet.

"Where did he go?" Officer Gilbert yells.

"Either out of the house or down to the basement," I say, already starting for the basement.

Another two shots are fired.

"No!" I scream as I take off for the basement.

"Piper!" Dad yells after me.

Everything is a blur as I race down the stairs. There on the floor are Mitchell and Officer Andrews. Both have blood in the center of their foreheads. I fall to my knees beside Mitchell.

"He went out the window," Officer Wallace yells into his radio.

"I've got him," Officer Gilbert calls back.

"Mitchell," I sob. "Mitchell, look at me." I turn his face toward me. "You can't leave me. Please don't leave me. I love you."

"Piper," Dad says, trying to pull me away. "Piper, open your eyes."

I do, and I see things clearly. Mitchell wasn't shot in the forehead. It's just a cut. I search him for a wound.

"The bullet only grazed my shoulder. He shot at us

while he tried to escape through the window," Mitchell says.

"You're okay?" I ask.

He nods. "You're wearing my shirt as a dress," Mitchell says.

I laugh. "You don't want to see what I was wearing before this. Trust me when I say this is a thousand times better."

"We have an officer down," Officer Wallace says into his radio.

I turn to get a better look at Officer Andrews. He wasn't as lucky as Mitchell. There's blood all over the front of his shirt.

"I need an ambulance at 1412 Montgomery Street. Now!" Officer Wallace yells.

I watch as Officer Wallace starts administering life saving techniques. Applying pressure to stop the bleeding.

"What happened?" I ask Mitchell.

"We both tried to stop the killer. That's why he shot at us. Andrews pushed me out of the way with his shoulder. I collided with the cement edge of the window and got knocked out for a second."

"That explains the gash on your head, but are you saying Officer Andrews saved your life?"

He nods again.

"Why?"

"I told you he was a good cop. You rattle him, but

when push comes to shove, he does his job and protects people."

Officer Andrews tried to fight the killer while still in handcuffs and saved Mitchell's life in the process. I can hardly believe it. "Can you sit up?" I ask Mitchell, since he's still lying down.

"My head's a little woozy, but I think so."

I help him sit up. "I'm assuming he took the keys to the handcuffs."

"Naturally." Mitchell is staring at Officer Andrews.

"Is there anything I can do?" I ask Officer Wallace.

"Yeah, can you keep applying pressure? I hear the ambulance. I want to bring them down here. Andrews is losing a lot of blood. We need to get him to the hospital fast."

I take over, pressing my hands to the wound the way Officer Wallace was.

The paramedics make quick work of getting downstairs with the gurney and loading Officer Andrews onto it. Once that's taken care of, Officer Wallace frees Mitchell from the handcuffs.

"You should get that shoulder looked at as well," he tells Mitchell.

"I'll drive him to the hospital," Dad says.

"On the way, you can explain to me why you're the worst boyfriend ever and went after a killer on your own without telling me," I say to Mitchell, crossing my arms in front of me.

He looks to Dad for help, but Dad holds up his hands and walks away.

————

Mitchell was too lightheaded on the drive to the hospital to talk, so I have to wait until after he's admitted and seen to by the doctor. Dad and I sit in the waiting room for two hours before the nurse agrees to let me see him for all of ten minutes. I must look as angry as I feel because she gives me a stern warning not to upset him.

I push open the door to his room. He's sitting up in bed with a bandage on his head and on his shoulder.

"Hey," he says.

"Hey yourself." I stand at the foot of the bed, not wanting to get any closer.

"You're still mad."

"Of course, I'm mad. How could I not be mad?" I cross my arms and look away from him so I don't accidentally feel bad for him since he's pretty banged up.

"I couldn't tell you what I did because I knew you'd be angry," Mitchell starts.

As soon as he says it, all the pieces start to fall into place. I face him with narrowed eyes. "Wait a second. You went to see Becky, didn't you? You sweet talked her into giving you Cole's information." I can't believe I actually started to like that woman and she never told me this. Even when I told her Mitchell was missing and in danger, she still didn't tell me he came to her or that she gave him Cole's address.

"Piper, please let me explain." He pats the bed next to him, but I'm not willing to give in that easily. I maintain my position. "Fine. Stand." He takes a deep breath before diving into his explanation. "Every case we work on together, you get all the leads and I follow you around. For once, I had a means of acquiring information you couldn't, and I jumped at the chance."

"And your stupid male ego almost got you killed," I say. "You should be so proud of that."

"I know I shouldn't have gone to the house. I should have gotten the address and waited until morning to pursue the lead."

"Exactly. So why didn't you? Why did you go off on your own?"

He smooths the bedcovers and avoids my eyes. "Because of my fragile male ego."

"Do you not like working with me?" I ask.

His head whips up. "What? No. Why would you even ask me that?"

"Because you deliberately followed a lead without me. You left me out. Completely. How else am I supposed to take that?"

He pats the bed again. "Please sit."

God, he's like a dog with the way his big eyes plead with me. I swear he learned that trick from Jez. I take two steps around the bed and sit.

"Do you know how hard it is to work with my girlfriend? Every time we walk into a dangerous situation, my first instinct is to protect you." He holds up a hand. "I know you don't need my protection, but I can't help wanting to keep you safe. It's no different than when you give your dad all the research aspects of the job to keep him out of danger."

I can't argue with him there. I do that to Dad all the time.

He reaches for my left hand and laces his fingers through mine. "I'm terrified of losing you."

"You're terrified? Do you realize what you put me through? I had visions of you being shot in the head. Or at least I thought that's what I was seeing." Now I know I was letting my fear cloud my visions. It wasn't a bullet hole. It was the cut from the window ledge.

"I had no idea. I'm so sorry."

"Then you're an idiot, Mitchell. You had to know I'd use my visions to find you. I read that stupid photograph of us from Christmas."

"Hey, I love that picture. It's the only picture I have of you, and you actually look happy to be with me."

"You were tickling me."

He squeezes my hand. "I'm sorry. I promise I'll never run off on my own like that again."

"You better not because I swear I won't put up with it."

"Understood."

The door opens, and the nurse walks in tapping her watch. "You're on overtime. He needs his rest. He's on concussion watch."

I don't bother arguing. "Get some rest," I tell him as I stand up.

"Thanks for rescuing me," he says.

"That's what girlfriends are for, right?" I smile and close the door behind me.

"He'll be discharged in the morning if you want to pick him up," the nurse tells me.

"Thanks. I will. Can you tell me how the other police officer is doing? Kurt Andrews?"

She shakes her head. "Sorry, but I can only disclose that information to immediate family members."

"Is his wife here?" I ask her.

She points to the corner of the waiting room. "She could probably use a friend."

Unfortunately for Angela, she only has me. I walk over to her and sit down. "Can I get you anything? I cup of really bad hospital coffee maybe?"

She laughs, but it's forced. "He got lucky. The bullet just missed his lungs. I just knew something like this would happen one day. I warned him. He has no idea how difficult it is to be the wife of a cop." She meets my gaze. "Don't ever marry a police officer. Ever. The constant fear and not knowing where he is..."

"My father was a police detective, so I know what you mean," I tell her.

"Is he retired?" she asks.

"Yes, he works with me now, although I'm not sure that's any safer."

She dabs her eyes with a tissue and pulls a watch from her purse. "You're psychic. Will you do me a favor and read this to tell me if Kurt will be okay?"

I still can't have visions of the future at will. They have to just come to me. "I'm afraid seeing the future isn't my strong suit."

"You've read him before, haven't you?" she surprises me by asking.

"What makes you think that?"

"I can tell he's not fond of you, so I assume that means you know more about him than he wants you to." She sniffles and wipes her nose with the tissue. "He's a private man."

I've always thought Angela has a right to know about her husband's activities outside of their marriage, but after he saved Mitchell's life today, I feel like I owe him something in return.

"He's having an affair, isn't he?" she asks, surprising me a little since I didn't think she had a clue.

I don't want to lie to her, so I choose my words carefully. "Mrs. Andrews, your husband doesn't like me because I was able to solve cases he couldn't. I made him look bad, and I'm the reason he was suspended from the force for a while."

"Suspended? He told me he was helping out at the academy, training new recruits."

At least I can tell her a small truth. "He lied, most likely because he was embarrassed to tell you the truth. But I can also tell you that the reason why he's fighting for his life right now is because he saved a fellow police officer today. He's a hero."

Her body shudders with sobs. "Thank you."

I nod and stand up.

Dad meets me at the nurses' desk. "That was a nice thing you did back there."

"I couldn't rat him out. Not after he saved Mitchell's life. His wife deserves better, but I just couldn't tell her the truth."

"I know, pumpkin. And sometimes, brushes with death like this can change a person."

I sense change in Officer Andrews's future, but I don't think it's the kind Dad is implying.

CHAPTER TWENTY

"I appreciate you coming down here this morning, Ashwell," Chief Johansen says, leaning back in his chair and turning his pen end over end on the top of his desk. "I understand Mitchell is being release today."

"Yes, sir. I'm going to pick him up after we're done here."

"I've always known he had a tendency to look the other way when you didn't follow protocol, but I never thought he'd do it himself."

"Neither did I, and I can assure you I've had a long talk with him about that subject."

He chuckles. "I'm sure you did. But I should tell you that I'm going to be making some changes around here, and if I find out either of you is breaking the rules, you'll find yourself back in this office and having a very different kind of conversation with me. Am I making myself clear?"

"Crystal." He's going to be watching us like a hawk, which is going to make following my leads harder than it's ever been before. Then something else he said registers. "What kind of changes should I expect?"

"For one, you won't be seeing Officer Andrews around here anymore."

"What? Why?"

"I told you either Andrews or Brennan would be reassigned. I've chosen Andrews—once he recovers, that is."

"You know he saved Mitchell's life, right?"

He nods. "I'm well aware of that fact."

"Then why are you punishing him? If you think you're doing me a favor by—"

He holds up a hand to stop me. "Ashwell, I trust your ability to help out this police force, but I'm not in the business of doing people favors. I'm doing what's best for this department and this town. Understood?"

"Understood."

"Good. Now go bring Mitchell home, and tell him to call me and update me on how long he'll be recuperating."

"I will." I get up and walk out of the office.

"Piper," Officer Wallace says, waving me over to his desk. "I was hoping I'd see you."

"What's up?" I ask.

"I thought you'd want to know that the killer's name is Carson Zelinski. Cole Bailey started renting a room from him about three weeks ago when he moved into town.

Bailey was a real people person, which is pretty much the complete opposite of Zelinski. But Zelinski soon learned Bailey was a great source of information since people tended to tell him their life stories."

"Did Zelinski tell you this?" I ask, curious if they were able to get a confession out of him.

"Yup. All of it. He's actually proud of himself. It's sick, but it makes our job easier. He's pleading guilty to theft, abduction, and murder."

"So Cole really had no idea his roommate was using him for information?"

"Nope. Zelinski called Bailey," he pauses, trying to remember the exact words, "a bigger moron than any meathead he'd ever met."

"I guess he doesn't have a high opinion of weightlifters."

"Could be jealousy. Zelinski had to use a gun to throw his weight around, if you know what I mean."

"I do. I've always thought it was a coward's weapon." I meet his gaze. "No offense. I know you guys all carry guns."

He laughs. "No worries, Piper. I know what you mean. Are you off to pick up Brennan?"

"Yeah, I am." I motion to the door. "Hey, before I go, I'm just curious how everyone's taking the news of Officer Andrews being transferred."

He leans over the desk and whispers, "No one is sorry to see him go. It's kind of sad if you ask me."

I nod. It is sad. And I can't help wondering if a lot of that has to do with me.

"Give Brennan my best," Officer Wallace says.

"I will." I wave and head to the hospital.

Mitchell is still in the process of being discharged, so I check on Officer Andrews. I spot his wife coming out of his room, so I know he's out of critical condition. Still, he was given a private room, which means his road to recovery will be long. I look around for any sign of the nurses who might tell me I can't visit because I'm not immediate family. I don't spot any, so I duck into the room.

Officer Andrews is hooked up to a monitor that's beeping steadily. His eyes are closed, but he looks older somehow. Like maybe the experience aged him. His chest is bandaged, but I can see the steady rise and fall of his breathing. I'm turning to leave and let him sleep when his eyes open.

"What are you doing here?" he asks in a groggy voice.

"I wanted to see how you were doing."

"Peachy," he answers.

I nod. "I can see." I'm not sure where to start. I want to thank him, apologize to him, and tell him what a jerk he is all at the same time. I settle on something I haven't been able to figure out about the case. "Are you the reason the Carson Zelinski found out about me and tried to frame me? I mean, were you complaining about me to Cole at the gym."

"That's entirely possible. Are you looking for an apology? Because that's not going to happen."

"No. Nothing like that. You had no way of knowing it would lead to Zelinski trying to frame me for murder."

"I think he was willing to pin this on you or Isaiah Young."

He's right. Zelinski faked those emails to point blame in two different directions, both completely away from him. "I see you've been debriefed on the case."

He nods. "Angela said you talked to her."

"I didn't tell her. I'm not going to. It's between the two of you."

"You don't owe me any favors."

"I kind of do." I step closer to the bed. "Mitchell told me what you did. How you saved his life."

"I did my job."

"He's not your partner. You didn't have to take a bullet for him."

"Maybe I was just trying to prove I'm a better cop than he is."

I laugh. "Now that sounds more like something you'd do."

He tries to laugh, but he cringes.

"Sorry."

"I don't want your pity, Ashwell. I don't want anything from you."

"I know, but I have to apologize."

"For being a total pain in my ass?" he asks. When I

don't respond, he says, "Oh, you think you're the cause of my transfer." He tries to sit up a little. "Look. Don't go thinking you drove me out of here, Ashwell. You don't get the credit for that. I'm leaving because I want to. I'll admit when the chief first brought up a transfer, I wanted to stay just to stick it to you and Brennan, the happy couple. But the truth is, I've wanted to get out of this town. It's too small for me. Everyone knows everyone else's business."

I can see how that would be bad for him. "You want a fresh start," I say.

"Don't go reading me."

"Sorry. That one sort of just came to me. It's the energy you're giving off."

"Then it's definitely time for you to leave. I can't say I'm going to miss you."

"Right back at you." I turn, but I pause in the doorway. "Even still, I wish you the best of luck in Tillboro Hills. And if you ever run into Madison Kramer, the thriller author, be nice to her. She's almost as insightful as I am." I had the pleasure of meeting Maddie on a previous case, and she and I really hit it off. Part of me feels I should warn her that Officer Andrews will be invading her town.

"Wonderful. It's just my luck I'd get transferred somewhere you actually have a friend."

"Considering how few friends I have, that really is awful luck." I walk out and down the hallway to Mitchell's room.

He's being wheeled out just as I reach the door. "Hey, you. I thought you forgot about me."

"I keep trying, but I haven't been able to forget you yet, Detective," I tease.

He reaches for my hand. "Will you please tell Nurse Hard-ass that I'm fine to walk out of this place on my own?"

"For the last time, Detective Brennan, my name is Nurse Harding. And it's hospital policy to wheel you out, so if you'll stop complaining, we can get you out of here and out of my hair." She immediately starts pushing him toward the elevators.

I lean down and whisper, "I can't believe we actually found a woman you can't charm."

"Nah. She loves me. She's just putting on a show so you don't get jealous." He winks.

I roll my eyes. "Sure, she is."

Once we're outside, I pull my Mazda up to the pickup area, and Nurse Harding hurries away the second Mitchell is in the passenger seat.

"Are we heading to the office?" Mitchell asks me.

"No. I'm taking you home. Dad is handling the background check we have on our plate so I can make sure you get some rest."

"Aw, I don't want to go home. Take me to your place instead. Jezebel is probably a great therapy dog. She'll have me feeling a hundred percent in no time."

"Are you using your injuries to get an invite to my apartment?" I ask, giving him the side-eye.

"Hey, you stayed at my place while I was being held hostage in that basement. It's only fair."

"Fine, but you should take my bed since you're recovering. I'll take the couch."

"No way. Your couch is super comfy, and besides, Jez is a cover hog. You've told me so."

I laugh. "That she is."

I get Mitchell settled on the couch, but truth be told, he seems fine. The cut on his head is healing, and the bullet barely grazed his shoulder. The guys at the station even made fun of him for being a baby about it because you can hardly see where he was shot. He did take two hits to the head, though, so I want him to relax and take it easy for a few days.

"I can order food if you're hungry," I tell him.

"I'm not hungry right now. Come sit with me." He moves his legs to make room for me on the couch.

I sit down, and Jez jumps up beside me. She's been careful not to be as "loving" to Mitchell as usual. I think she can sense he's hurt, and her kisses are sometimes a little too powerful when she has trouble containing her excitement. No one gets her more excited than Mitchell. She really does love him.

"Do you want to watch TV?" I ask, reaching for the remote on the coffee table.

"Do you even know how to turn it on?" he teases.

"Ha-ha, Mr. Comedian. I'm going to read my book, so it's not going to affect me if I leave the remote over here where you can't reach it."

"I thought we could just hang out and talk. You did go almost two days without talking to me. I'm assuming you missed the sound of my voice." He smirks.

"You're so full of yourself, Detective. I'm surprised you're not telling me you would have found a way to rescue yourself if I didn't show up."

"I probably would have, but it was fun seeing you show up wearing my shirt."

"Fun? There was nothing fun about any of that."

"One good thing came out of all of this," Mitchell says, pulling me toward him on the couch so I can settle between his outstretched legs.

"What's that?" I lean back against his chest.

"You admitted you love me."

"I think those hits you took to the head made you delusional, Detective."

He laughs. "Deny it all you want. I know what I heard."

"You heard what you wanted to hear."

"That might be true, but it's also what you said and what you feel." He kisses the top of my head. "Jez isn't the only female in this apartment who loves me anymore."

Jez picks her head up and stares at Mitchell.

"Don't worry. You're still my favorite," he whispers to her.

I smile. "I wouldn't dream of trying to come between you two."

He leans his chin on my shoulder. "I wouldn't dream of letting anyone come between you and me."

"Not even Becky?" I ask, turning my face toward his.

"Speaking of *Becky*." He picks up his head. "Gilbert told me an interesting story when he stopped by the hospital yesterday."

Oh, good Lord. "I'm going to kill him."

Mitchell laughs. "You posed as a stripper to come to my rescue?"

"I did what I had to do, and besides, it wasn't my idea."

"Do you still have the outfit?"

I palm my forehead. "I left it at your place when I changed into your shirt."

He laughs again. "This just keeps getting better and better. You really know how to cheer up a guy when he's recovering."

"Yeah, yeah."

"I want that photo of us back, too," he says. "I know you kept it."

"I never should have let you have it in the first place."

"You can't take it back. It was a Christmas present. My favorite Christmas present, in fact."

"Fine. You can have it back since I'm never posing for another picture like that one again."

"We'll see. I'm sure you never thought you'd apply for a job as a stripper either, but look at you now!"

"I hope all this laughing at my expense gives you a headache."

"Why? Are you trying to keep me here longer so you can play nurse?"

"You're impossible. Do you know that? I should have left you to fend for yourself in that basement."

"But you didn't. Because you love me." He draws out the word "love."

Dear God help me because he's right. Not that I'm going to tell him that again anytime soon.

———

If you enjoyed the book, please consider leaving a review. And look for *A Vision in Time Saves Nine* coming soon!

Stay up-to-date on all of Kelly's releases by subscribing to her newsletter: https://bit.ly/2ISdgCU

ALSO BY USA TODAY BESTSELLING AUTHOR KELLY HASHWAY

Piper Ashwell Psychic P.I. Series

A Sight For Psychic Eyes

A Vision A Day Keeps the Killer Away

Read Between the Crimes

Drastic Crimes Call for Drastic Insights

You Can't Judge a Crime by its Aura

Fortune Favors the Felon

Murder is a Premonition Best Served Cold

It's Beginning to Look a Lot Like Murder

Good Visions Make Good Cases (Novella collection)

A Jailbird in the Vision Is Worth Two In The Prison

Great Crimes Read Alike

I Spy With My Psychic Eye Someone Dead

A Vision in Time Saves Nine

Never Smite the Psychic That Reads You

There's No Crime Like the Prescient

Fight Fire With Foresight

Madison Kramer Mystery Series

Manuscripts and Murder

Sequels and Serial Killers

Fiction and Felonies

Cup of Jo

Coffee and Crime

Macchiatos and Murder

Cappuccinos and Corpses

Frappes and Fatalities

Lattes and Lynching

Glaces and Graves

Espresso and Evidence

Paranormal Books:

Touch of Death (Touch of Death #1)

Stalked by Death (Touch of Death #2)

Face of Death (Touch of Death #3)

The Monster Within (The Monster Within #1)

The Darkness Within (The Monster Within #2)

Unseen Evil (Unseen Evil #1)

Evil Unleashed (Unseen Evil #2)

Into the Fire (Into the Fire #1)

Out of the Ashes (Into the Fire #2)

Up in Flames (Into the Fire #3)

Dark Destiny

Fading Into the Shadows

The Day I Died

Replica

ACKNOWLEDGMENTS

At this point, I probably sound like a broken record, but I have the best team to work with on these books. Patricia Bradley, you're amazing to work with and you keep my writing the best it possibly can be. Thank you for your continued enthusiasm for Piper and Mitchell. To my cover designer, Ali Winters at Red Umbrella Graphic Designs, I have so much fun working with you on each cover, and you make it so difficult to choose a favorite cover for the series because they're all so amazing.

To my readers, my VIP reader group Kelly's Cozy Corner, and my ARC readers, thank you for giving me a reason to keep writing more stories in this series. And to my family, thank you for the never-ending support and interest in what I love to do.

ABOUT THE AUTHOR

Kelly Hashway fully admits to being one of the most accident-prone people on the planet, but luckily she gets to write about female sleuths who are much more coordinated than she is. Maybe it was growing up watching *Murder, She Wrote* that instilled a love of mystery, but she spends her days writing cozy mysteries. Kelly's also a sucker for first love, which is why she writes romance under the pen name Ashelyn Drake. When she's not writing, Kelly works as an editor and also as Mom, which she believes is a job title that deserves to be capitalized.

 facebook.com/KellyHashwayCozyMysteryAuthor

 twitter.com/kellyhashway

instagram.com/khashway

bookbub.com/authors/kelly-hashway